AF575165

A Child's Place

HARCOURT BRACE SOCIAL STUDIES

Series Authors

Dr. Richard G. Boehm

Claudia Hoone

Dr. Thomas M. McGowan

Dr. Mabel C. McKinney-Browning

Dr. Ofelia B. Miramontes

Dr. Priscilla H. Porter

Series Consultants

Dr. Alma Flor Ada

Dr. Phillip Bacon

Dr. W. Dorsey Hammond

Dr. Asa Grant Hilliard, III

HARCOURT BRACE & COMPANY

Orlando Atlanta Austin Boston San Francisco Chicago Dallas

New York Toronto London

 Visit The Learning Site at http://www.hbschool.com

Series Authors

Dr. Richard G. Boehm
Professor and Jesse H. Jones Distinguished Chair in Geographic Education
Department of Geography and Planning
Southwest Texas State University
San Marcos, Texas

Claudia Hoone
Teacher
Ralph Waldo Emerson School #58
Indianapolis, Indiana

Dr. Thomas M. McGowan
Associate Professor
Division of Curriculum and Instruction
Arizona State University
Tempe, Arizona

Dr. Mabel C. McKinney-Browning
Director
Division for Public Education
American Bar Association
Chicago, Illinois

Dr. Ofelia B. Miramontes
Associate Professor of Education and Associate Vice Chancellor for Diversity
University of Colorado
Boulder, Colorado

Dr. Priscilla H. Porter
Co-Director
Center for History–Social Science Education
School of Education
California State University, Dominguez Hills
Carson, California

Series Consultants

Dr. Alma Flor Ada
Professor
School of Education
University of San Francisco
San Francisco, California

Dr. Phillip Bacon
Professor Emeritus of Geography and Anthropology
University of Houston
Houston, Texas

Dr. W. Dorsey Hammond
Professor of Education
Oakland University
Rochester, Michigan

Dr. Asa Grant Hilliard, III
Fuller E. Callaway Professor of Urban Education
Georgia State University
Atlanta, Georgia

Media, Literature, and Language Specialists

Dr. Joseph A. Braun, Jr.
Professor of Elementary Social Studies
Department of Curriculum and Instruction
Illinois State University
Normal, Illinois

Meredith McGowan
Youth Services Librarian
Tempe Public Library
Tempe, Arizona

Rebecca Valbuena
Language Development Specialist
Stanton Elementary School
Glendora, California

Grade-Level Consultants

Barbara Abbott
Adams Elementary School
San Diego, California

Janice Bell
Hammel Street Elementary School
Los Angeles, California

Carol Hamilton Cobb
Gateway School
Metropolitan Nashville Public Schools
Madison, Tennessee

Janet J. Eubank
Language Arts Curriculum Specialist
Wichita Public Schools
Wichita, Kansas

Billie M. Kapp
Teacher (Retired)
Coventry Grammar School
Coventry, Connecticut

Amy Keller
Resource Teacher
Orange County Public Schools
Orlando, Florida

Carol Siefkin
Garfield Elementary School
Carmichael, California

Grade-Level Reviewers

Bonnie A. Coss
Jacksonville Heights Elementary School
Jacksonville, Florida

Trudy Ellis
Park Hills Elementary School
Spartanburg, South Carolina

Kimberly Gay
Mango Elementary School
Seffner, Florida

Dolores Hudson
Frontier Elementary School
Clearwater, Florida

Donna Lewis
Frances S. Tucker Elementary School
Coconut Grove, Florida

Betty Maxey
W. H. Taft Elementary School
Boise, Idaho

Mildred S. McCarthy
Atkins Technology Elementary School
Shreveport, Louisiana

Pam I. Moore
Rincon Elementary School
Rincon, Georgia

Barbara E. Oglesby
Paloma Elementary School
Temecula, California

Nan Pelletier
Boise Public Schools
Boise, Idaho

Michelle Rose
Mary Tsukamoto Elementary School
Sacramento, California

Susan Young
S. L. Lewis Elementary School
College Park, Georgia

Acknowledgments and other credits appear in the back of this book.

Printed in the United States of America

ISBN 0-15-318373-X

2 3 4 5 6 7 8 9 10 032 2004 2003 2002 2001

Contents

At Home with My Family

UNIT 3

Living in a Community

UNIT 4

In and Around the Land

UNIT 6

My World Near and Far

F.Y.I.

Literature and Primary Sources

Skills

Features

Biography

Brainstorm

Making Social Studies Real

Maps

Charts, Graphs, Diagrams, Tables, and Time Lines

Atlas

Geo Georgie invites you to visit new places this year. The maps in this book will help you find your way. When you see Geo Georgie, stop and learn how to use the maps.

Come back to this Atlas often as you travel. It will help you see where you are!

Atlas

The World

ARCTIC OCEAN

EUROPE

ASIA

PACIFIC OCEAN

AFRICA

INDIAN OCEAN

AUSTRALIA

ATLANTIC OCEAN

N
W
E
S

ANTARCTICA

Atlas

The United States

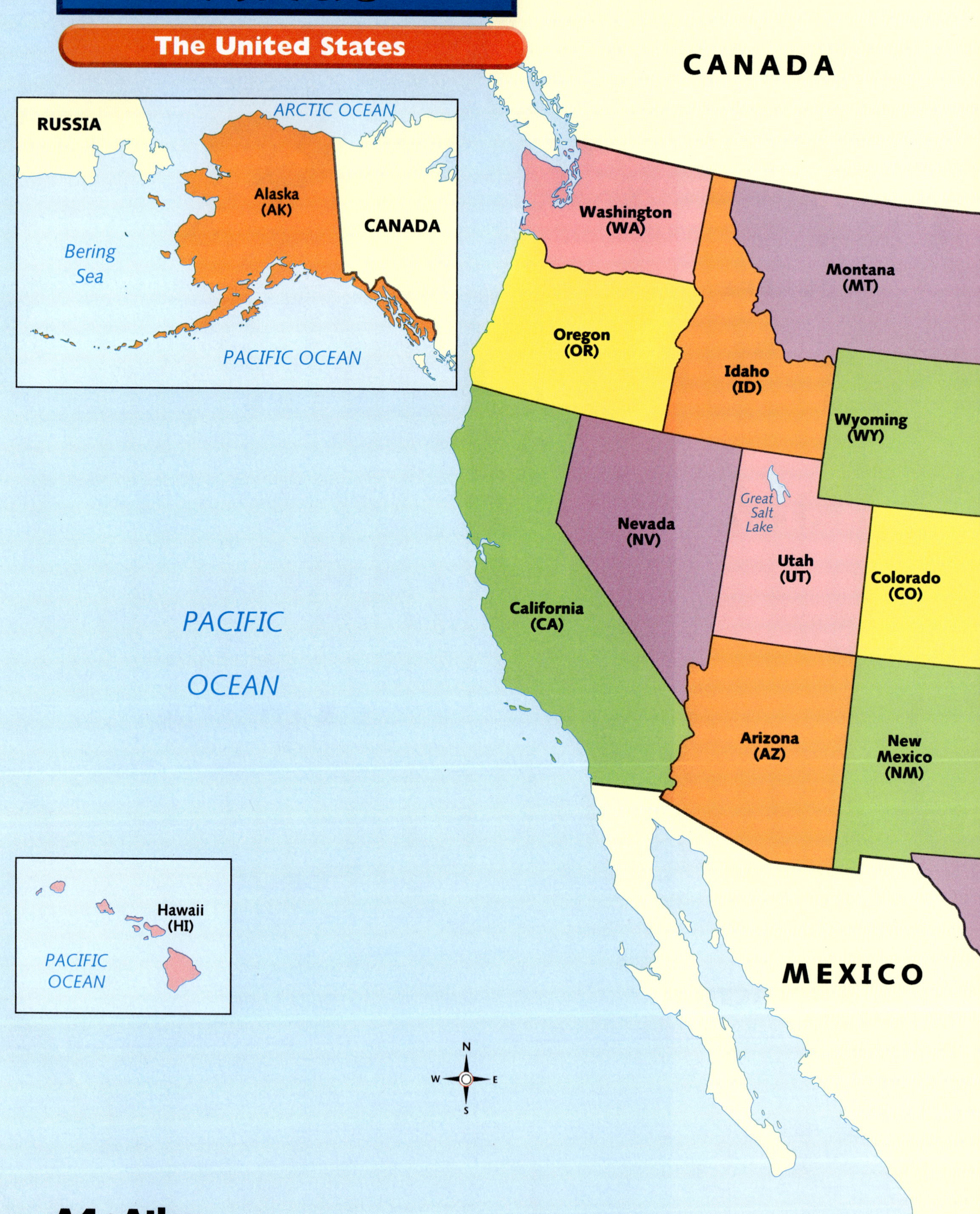

CANADA
Lake Superior
Lake Huron
Lake Michigan
Lake Ontario
Lake Erie
North Dakota (ND)
Minnesota (MN)
South Dakota (SD)
Wisconsin (WI)
Michigan
(MI)
Nebraska (NE)
Iowa (IA)
Illinois (IL)
Indiana (IN)
Ohio (OH)
Kansas (KS)
Missouri (MO)
Kentucky (KY)
West Virginia (WV)
Virginia (VA)
Oklahoma (OK)
Arkansas (AR)
Tennessee (TN)
North Carolina (NC)
South Carolina (SC)
Texas (TX)
Louisiana (LA)
Mississippi (MS)
Alabama (AL)
Georgia (GA)
Florida (FL)
Maine (ME)
Vermont (VT)
New Hampshire (NH)
New York (NY)
Massachusetts (MA)
Rhode Island (RI)
Connecticut (CT)
Pennsylvania (PA)
New Jersey (NJ)
Maryland (MD)
Delaware (DE)
Washington, D.C.
ATLANTIC OCEAN
Gulf of Mexico

UNIT 1

School Days

Vocabulary

school
teacher
map
group
rule

SCHOOL BUS
INTER

Unit 1 Preview

school

MIDDLETON HEIGHTS ELEMENTARY

teacher

map

group

Class Rules

Stand in line.

Raise your hand.

Be quiet in the library.

Don't chew gum.

First Day of School

by Aileen Fisher

illustrated by Stacey Schuett

I wonder
if my drawing
will be as good as theirs.

I wonder
if they'll like me
or just be full of stares.

I wonder
if my teacher
will look like Mom or Gram.

I wonder
if my puppy
will wonder
where I am.

LESSON

I Learn at School

2. title

I learn to read at school. To **learn** is to find out something new.

3. new word

1. lesson number

I learn about children far away.

4. picture

I learn how to get along with others.

What Do You Know?

How do pictures and words help you learn?

LESSON

My Classroom

My classroom is where I learn at **school**. I read in my classroom. I write there, too. My teacher helps me learn.

What Do You Know?

What would you say in a letter about school?

Learn from a Picture and a Map

A **map** is a drawing. It shows what a place would look like if you could see it from above.

Look at this picture of a classroom.

Skills

2 This is a picture of the same classroom from above.

3 Look at a map of the classroom.

Think and Do

What do you see on the map? Make a list.

LESSON

School Workers

We all work at school. Each person has a **job** to do.

principal

custodian

server

What Do You Know?

What is your job at school?

Read a Map Key

A **map key** is a list of the symbols on a map.

A **symbol** is a picture that stands for something real. A map key tells what each symbol means.

1. Look at the map key.
2. Find the symbol for the office in the map key.
3. Where is the office on the map?

Map Key

gym

library

classroom

cafeteria

office

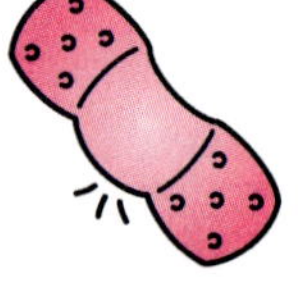
nurse

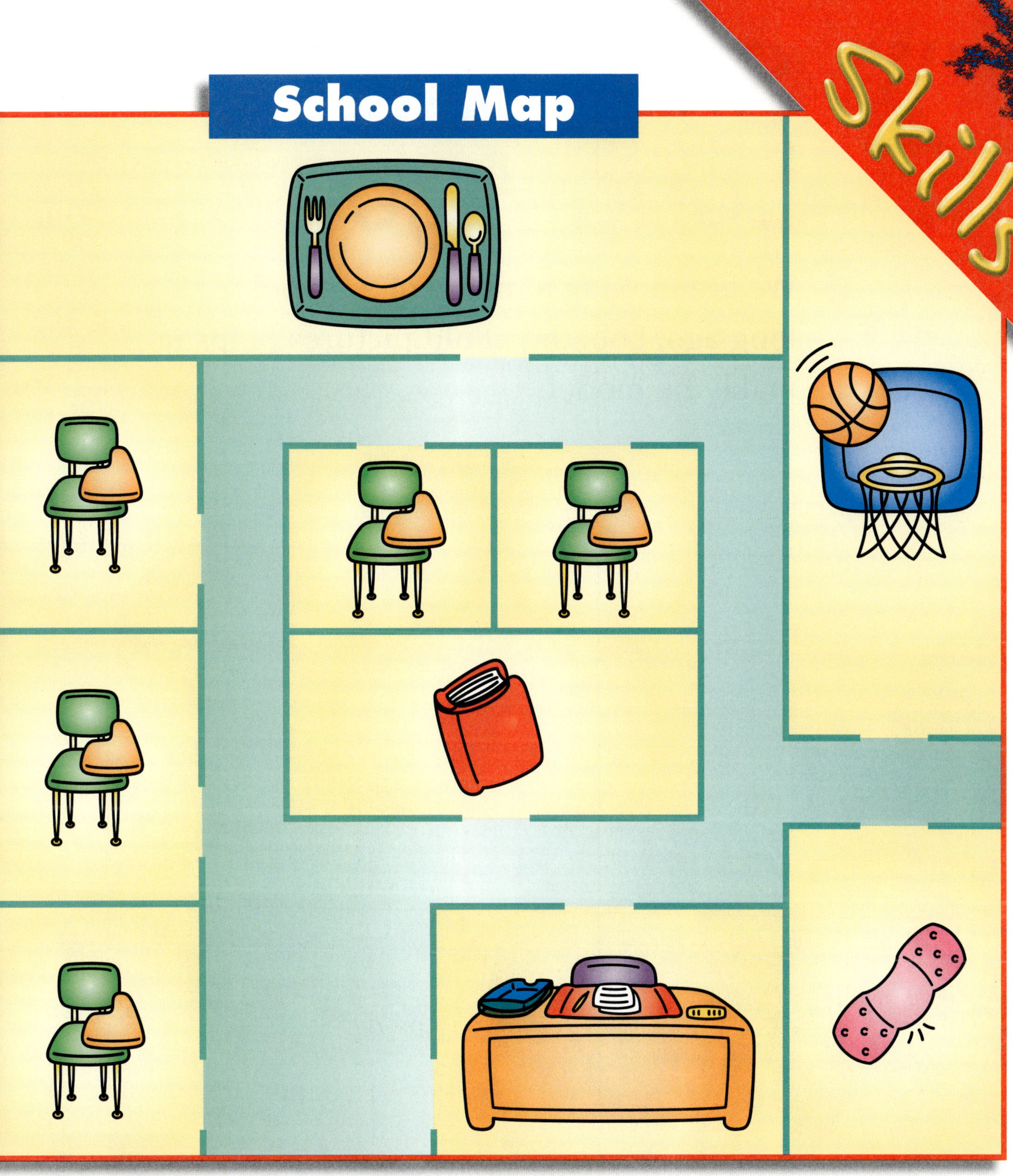

Think and Do

Tell how you would go from the office to the cafeteria.

LESSON 4

Schools Long Ago

We are making a model of a school from long ago. Looking at old pictures helps us make the model.

"New England Country School" by Winslow Homer

Long ago, most children walked to school. Some rode in a school wagon.

Children went to schools that had only one room. Schools did not have much paper. Children wrote on blackboards.

Schools did not have many books. Children learned from books like this one. They also read books from home.

History

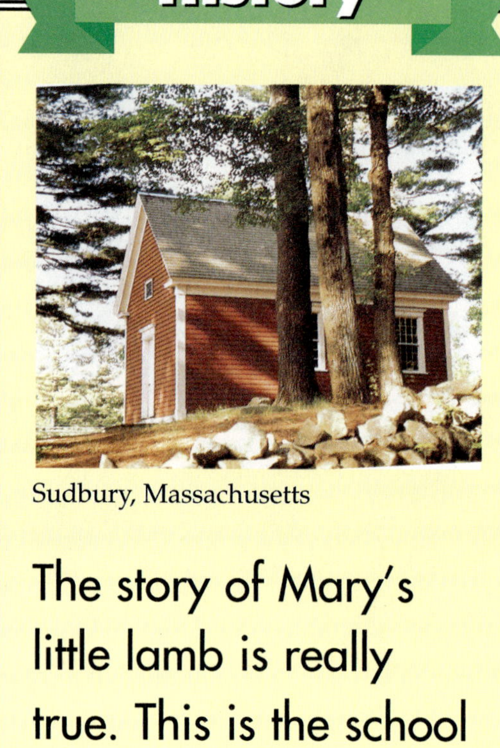

Sudbury, Massachusetts

The story of Mary's little lamb is really true. This is the school where Mary's lamb followed her.

70

ECLECTIC SERIES.

I think Henry is kind, for his sister is too small to skate.

Look! Did you see that boy ll down? But I see he is not t, for he is laughing.

me other boys have just to join in the sport. See put on their skates.

y says, that he hopes his ill get a pair of skates ister next winter.

paw mēans is n't spēak sĩr shāke Fī'dō trĭcks tēach dĭn'ner El'len bow'wow

Ellen, do look at Fido! He sits up in a chair, with my hat on. He looks like a little boy; but it is only Fido.

Now see him shake hands. Give me your paw, Fido. How do you do, sir? Will you take dinner with us, Fido? Speak!

On warm days children ate lunch outside. They carried their lunches in buckets or baskets. After lunch children liked to play circle games, marbles, and jump rope.

Today you can visit a one-room school. There you can see what it was like to go to school long ago.

What Do YOU Know?

How are schools today different from schools long ago?

LESSON

We Help One Another

We all have jobs to do in our classroom.

Some children work alone. Some children work together in a **group**. One group is making a scrapbook of our jobs.

What Do *You* Know?

What jobs would you show in a scrapbook about your class?

Solving Problems

Using Good Manners

Showing good manners is important. A person who has good manners is nice to be with. Being kind to others shows that you have good manners. Playing fair shows good manners, too.

Brainstorm

- Joey is new in school. What problem does he have?
- How do you think Joey feels?

What Would You Do?

- How would you solve this problem?
- What are some ways to use good manners? Make a list.

LESSON

We Follow School Rules

A **rule** tells us what we should or should not do. Read this class list.

Class Rules

Stand in line.

Raise your hand.

Be quiet in the library.

Don't chew gum.

Look at the pictures. Who is following a rule? Who is not?

What Do *You* Know?

What rules would you add to the list?

Kindness Counts

Hi! My name is Peter. I live in Lenexa, Kansas. My school has a program called Kindness Is Contagious. We show kindness to others.

One day my class skipped recess. We went into another classroom while that class was playing outside. We washed their desks and cleaned up their room.

Another class picked up trash on the playground. It looked great!

Rescue workers needed stuffed animals to give to children. We gave them more than 100 stuffed animals!

Being kind has made our school a happier place. Kindness could make the world a happier place, too!

What Can You Do?

- Start a Kindness Program in your classroom.
- List some ways to show kindness to others. Try some.

Picture Summary

Look at the pictures. They will help you remember what you learned.

Talk About the Main Ideas

1. Children learn many new things in their classrooms.
2. School workers and children have important jobs at school.
3. Working together and following rules helps get jobs done.
4. Schools today are different from schools long ago.

Tell a Story Choose one of the rooms. Make up a story about the people in the room. Share your story with the class.

Use Vocabulary

Tell which word goes with each picture.

teacher school group map rule

1 

2 

3 

4 

5 

Check Understanding

1. Tell one thing you learn in the classroom.
2. Name two school workers and tell what they do.
3. Tell one way schools today are different from schools long ago.
4. How does working in a group help get jobs done?

Think Critically

How do rules help you get along with others at home and at school?

Apply Skills

Read a Map Key

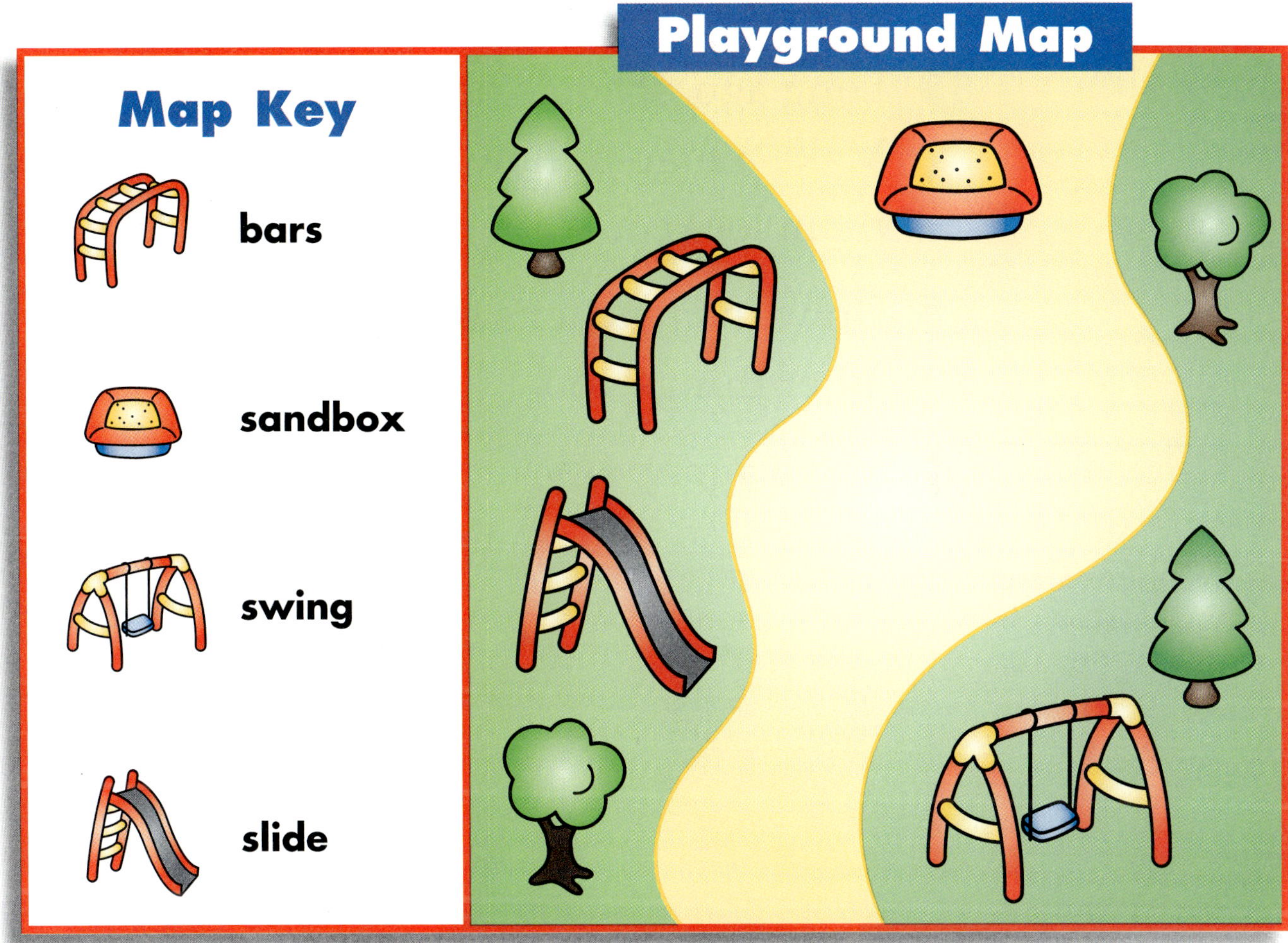

The map shows a playground. Use the map and map key to answer the questions.

1. What can you learn from the map key?
2. What is on the path between two trees?
3. What is between the bars and a tree?

Apply Skills

Do It Yourself

Make your own map and map key.

1. Long ago, schools had just one room. Make a map of how you think the room looked.
2. Draw the teacher's desk. Add some other things, too.
3. Make a map key.

Unit Activity

Make Classroom Award Ribbons

- Cut out a paper circle. Cut some paper ribbons, too.
- Write something about your class on the circle. Write some things you do together on the ribbons.
-  Glue the ribbons to the circle.

Visit the Internet at http://www.hbschool.com for additional resources.

Read More About It

The Little Red Hen by Patricia and Fredrick McKissack. Childrens Press. Meet a hen who wishes her friends would help her bake bread.

Never Spit on Your Shoes by Denys Cazet. Orchard. First graders help make their classroom rules.

Crow Boy by Taro Yashima. Puffin. A shy boy finds it hard to go to a new school.

UNIT

2

At Home with My Family

Vocabulary

family
change
money
choice
holiday

Unit 2 Preview

family

change

money

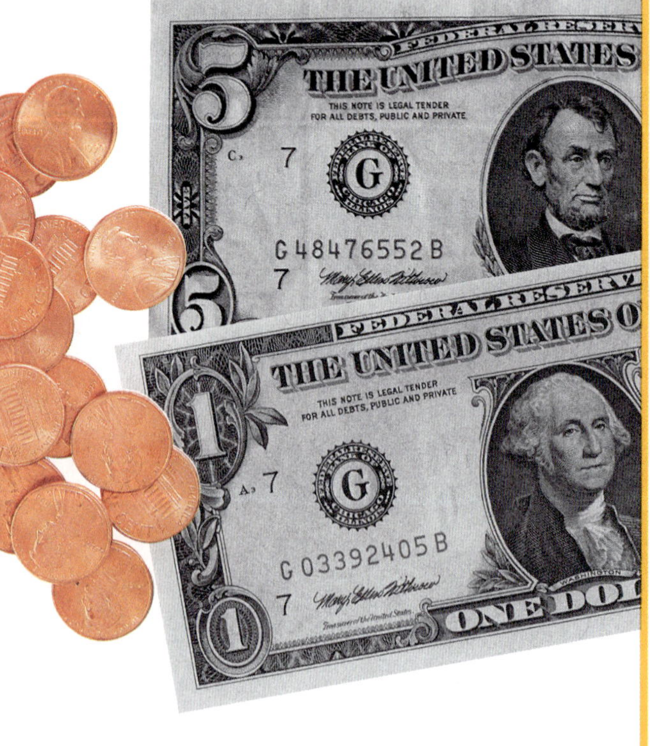

choice

holiday

Set the Scene with
Literature

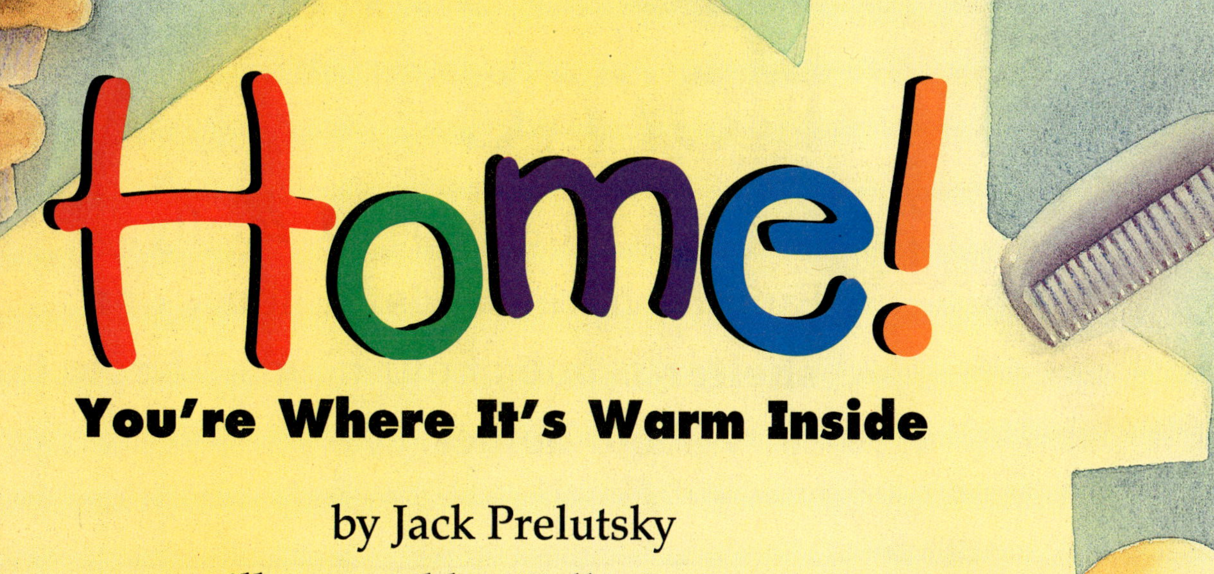

Home! You're Where It's Warm Inside

by Jack Prelutsky
illustrated by Holly Cooper

Home! You are a special place;
you're where I wake and wash my face,
brush my teeth and comb my hair,
change my socks and underwear,
clean my ears and blow my nose,
try on all my parents' clothes.

Home! You're where it's warm inside,
where my tears are gently dried,
where I'm comforted and fed,
where I'm forced to go to bed,
where there's always love to spare;
Home! I'm glad that you are there.

LESSON 1

Welcome Home

I live in a group. It is my **family**. Families have **needs**. A house or a **shelter** is one of our needs. I wrote this story about homes.

A nest is a home for a bird.

A doghouse is a home for Rusty.

A house is a home for some people. An **apartment** is a home for me.

What Do You Know?

What else do families need? Draw your family at home.

Find a Home Address on a Map

Homes have addresses. An **address** tells where a home is. The address has a house number and a street name.

1. Look at the map on page 49. What is the number of the blue house?

2. What is the name of the street?

Skills

Home Addresses

Think and Do

Point to the purple house on the map. What is the address?

The Leaving Morning

by ANGELA JOHNSON

illustrated by DAVID SOMAN

Families go through changes. A **change** is something new or different. Read how this family feels about moving.

The leaving happened on a soupy, misty morning, when you could hear the street sweeper.

Sssshhhshsh. . . .

We pressed our faces against the hall window and left cold lips on the pane.

It was the leaving morning. Boxes of clothes, toys, dishes, and pictures of us everywhere. The leaving had been long because we'd packed days before and said good-bye to everybody we knew. . . .

Our friends. . . .The grocer. . . .
Everybody in our building. . . .
And the cousins, especially
the cousins. We said good-bye
to the cousins all day long.

Mama said the people in a truck would move us and take care of everything we loved, on the leaving morning.

We woke up early and had hot cocoa from the deli across the street. I made more lips on the deli window and watched for the movers on the leaving morning.

We sat on the steps and watched the movers. They had blue moving clothes on and made bumping noises on the stairs. There were lots of whistles and "Watch out, kids."

Got me a moving hat and a kiss on the head from Miss Mattie, upstairs. And on the leaving morning she told me to watch myself in the new place when I crossed the street, and think of her.

I sat between my mama and daddy, holding their hands. My daddy said in a little while we'd be someplace we'd love.

So I left lips on the front window of our apartment, and said good-bye to our old place, on the leaving morning.

What Do YOU Know?

How is life changing for this family?

Chart and Graph Skills

Read a Time Line

In The Leaving Morning, you read about a family that is moving. Moving is a big change for a family. You can show changes on a time line. A **time line** shows when things happen. Look at Derrick's time line.

1. What happens first on the time line?
2. What happens next?
3. What happens last?

Learning to ride

Moving Day

3 years old	4 years old	5 years old	6 years old

Think and Do

Derrick lost his first tooth just before moving day. Where would the picture go on the time line?

LESSON 3

Families Make Choices

Families have wants. **Wants** are things people would like to have. Families use **money** to buy things they want. They must think about how to spend their money. They must also think about how to save their money.

I help my family shop. What we pick to buy is a **choice**. Choices help us meet our wants. There are five people in my family. Which box of cereal is the better choice?

What Do You Know?

What choices do families make?

Critical Thinking Skills

Make a Choice

Families cannot buy everything they want. They have to make choices. The Jones family is thinking about how to spend money wisely.

1. What does the family want?

2. What questions do they need to ask?

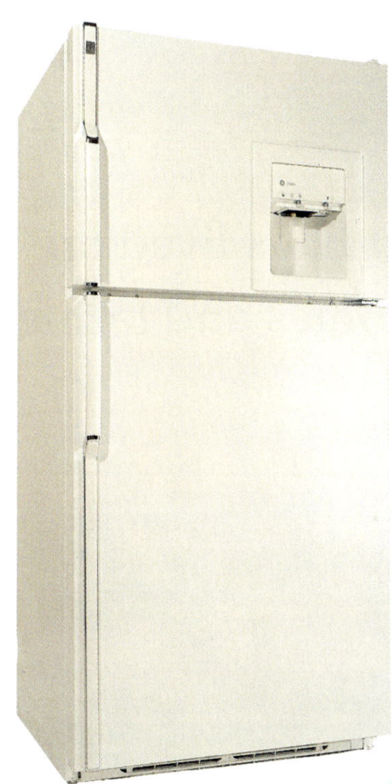

3 What will the family have to give up when they make their choice?

4 What choice do you think the family made?

Think and Do

Think of three things you want.
Tell how you would make a choice.

LESSON

Families Long Ago

A Thanksgiving Story

Long ago, only American Indians lived on this land. They built their homes and farmed the land.

Then people from far away began to come to America. These people were the Pilgrims. They wanted a new place to live.

They built homes and a village. American Indians showed the Pilgrims how to grow corn.

The Pilgrim families worked hard. Pilgrim children helped. Their plants grew, and they had a lot of food.

The Pilgrims wanted to **celebrate**. They invited the American Indians to share a special meal. They thanked God for all their food.

Today we remember the Pilgrims and the Indians on a **holiday** called Thanksgiving Day.

What Do You Know?

How does your family celebrate Thanksgiving?

Solving Problems

Tools from Long Ago

The Pilgrims used tools like these to make their Thanksgiving dinner. We can learn about the past by looking at things people used long ago. Work with a group. Look at the pictures.

- Make a chart.
- Write what you think each tool is.
- Write how you think it was used.

Show Your Ideas

- Tell what your group thinks about each tool.
- Tell why people look at tools from long ago to learn about the past.

Families Help Families

Hi! My name is Kaitlyn, and I have diabetes. I have to take a medicine called insulin. When I was seven, I read about a Russian boy named Ivan. He had diabetes but he could not get insulin.

I wanted to help Ivan. I wrote a letter to the President. His helpers called me! They gave my family and me some ideas. Then we found a way to get insulin to Ivan.

Dear President Clinton,

My name is Kaitlyn Bubb. I am seven and have had Juvenile Diabetes for more than 3 years. I am healthy because I have insulin, a good doctor, and good eating habits.

A lady

My family invited Ivan and his mother to visit. Ivan went to diabetes camp to learn how to stay well. He and I became friends.

Now I write to Ivan. His mother has started a group for families of children with diabetes. The families in my diabetes group help them. We are families helping families!

What Can You Do?

- Find out about a group in your community that helps families.
- Maybe your class can help.

Visit the Internet at http://www.hbschool.com for additional resources.

Picture Summary

Look at the pictures. They will help you remember what you learned.

Talk About the Main Ideas

1. Families have needs. One need is a home.
2. Families grow and change.
3. Families make choices about how to spend their money wisely.
4. Families long ago worked together, too.

Think Ahead What will a family be like 100 years from now? Draw a picture. Show how the family might be different from yours.

APPLES
49¢
BANAN

Use Vocabulary

Pat made a picture about one of these words.

money
choice
family
change
holiday

1. Which word is Pat's picture about?
2. Choose a different word. Make a picture about it.

Check Understanding

1. What are two things all families need?
2. How is a move a change for a family?
3. Why must families make choices about money?
4. Tell about a holiday your family likes.

Think Critically

How do people in a family show that they care about one another?

Apply Skills

Read a Time Line

Use the time line to answer these questions.

1. Whose birthday comes first?
2. In what month is Mom's birthday?
3. Does Brother's birthday come before or after Mom's?

Do It Yourself

Make your own birthday time line. Show your birthday on the time line. Show your family's birthdays, too.

Apply Skills

Find a Home Address on a Map

Draw your own map.

1. Draw a street. Write a name for the street.
2. Draw some houses. Write house numbers on them.
3. Trade maps with a classmate. Ask each other to find addresses on your maps.

Make a Choice

Imagine that you have 50 cents to spend at the store. You need a pencil for school. You want some stickers to give to your friends. You would like a snack. What should you buy?

- Choose what you think you should buy. Think about what might happen if you buy it.
- Think about what might happen if you do not buy it.

Unit Activity

Make a House

 Draw and cut out a big house.

 Cut out three squares and fold them in half. Make the squares look like a door and two windows.

 Draw a family inside the door. Draw things families need inside the windows.

 Paste the door and windows on the house.

Visit the Internet at http://www.hbschool.com for additional resources.

Read More About It

Houses and Homes by Ann Morris. Lothrop, Lee & Shepard. There are all kinds of houses!

Let's Eat! by Ana Zamorano. Scholastic. Someone is always missing from the dinner table in this home.

Over the River and Through the Wood by Lydia Maria Child. North-South Books. Ride along to Grandma's for Thanksgiving dinner.

UNIT

3

Living in a Community

Vocabulary

city
neighborhood
services
leader
goods

COMMUNITY
ALL STARS

Unit 3 Preview

city

neighborhood

services

leader

JEB BUSH
Florida's Governor

goods

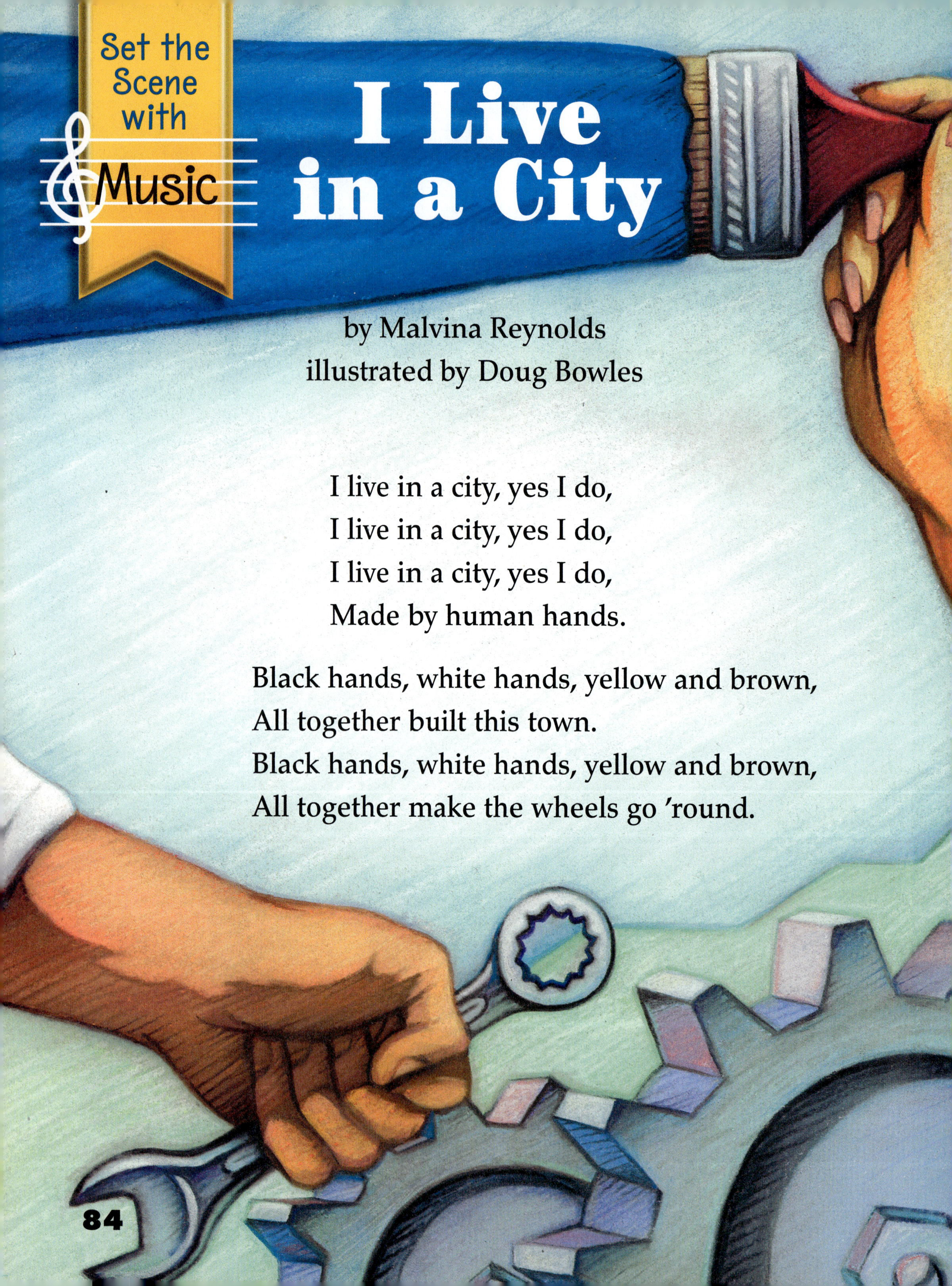

I Live in a City

by Malvina Reynolds
illustrated by Doug Bowles

I live in a city, yes I do,
I live in a city, yes I do,
I live in a city, yes I do,
Made by human hands.

Black hands, white hands, yellow and brown,
All together built this town.
Black hands, white hands, yellow and brown,
All together make the wheels go 'round.

Brown hands, yellow hands, white and black,
Mined the coal and built the stack.
Brown hands, yellow hands, white and black,
Built the engine and laid the track.

Black hands, white hands, brown and tan,
Milled the flour and cleaned the pan.
Black hands, white hands, brown and tan,
The working woman and the working man.

LESSON

Meet My Neighbors

A place where people live is a **community**. A **city** is a large community that has many **neighborhoods**. Read about the people who live in a city and its neighborhoods.

Hello, I'm Lisa. Welcome to my community. Come and meet some neighbors.

We buy bread from Mr. Ross.

Mr. Tims delivers our mail.
He brings mail to all the
people in my neighborhood.

Nikki is a tennis teacher. She teaches her students the rules of tennis. Rules make the game fair for everyone. Nikki also shows them how to be good sports. After each game, the winners and losers shake hands.

My mom works at a bank. A bank is a place to keep money. Our family saves money in the bank. We take some of the money out when we want to buy something.

Mr. Loomis takes care of our park. We like to ride our bikes in the park.

Officer Bob and Officer Dan work hard to keep our neighborhood safe.

What Do You Know?

1. Name three workers in Lisa's community.
2. What workers do you know in your community?

LESSON 2

The Post Office

Our class has pen pals in South Korea. We write letters to them about our community. They write letters to us about their community, too. Our letters go to the **post office**. The post office workers make sure our letters get to our pen pals.

1 The letters go to the post office.

2 The letters are sorted.

3 The letters are loaded on planes and flown to Korea.

History

The people shown on stamps have often done important things for our country. Abraham Lincoln and Harriet Tubman both worked to help people be free.

4 In South Korea, the letters are sorted again.

5 A mail carrier delivers the letters.

What Do You Know?

1. Where are the letters sorted?
2. What are some other ways to send letters?

LESSON

Community Leaders

Julio is talking to people about services. **Services** are jobs people do for others. Julio asked the mayor of Santa Ana, California, about his service job.

Julio: What does a mayor do?

Mayor Pulido: I am a community **leader**. My job is to serve the people of our city. I meet with other leaders of the city. We help run the community.

Julio: Where do you work?

Mayor Pulido: My office is in City Hall.

Julio: Why do you like being a mayor?

Mayor Pulido: I like making our city a better place to live.

What Do You Know?

1. What does a mayor do?
2. Who are the leaders in your community?

Find Directions on a Map

Maps can show where places are in a community. We use four **directions** to find places on a map. They are north, south, east, and west.

1. Find the North arrow on the map. Move your finger in the direction of the North arrow. You are going north.

2. Put your finger on Main Street. Move your finger from First Street to Third Street. You are going south.

3. Find East and West arrows on the map.

Map Key

apartments

house

park

city hall

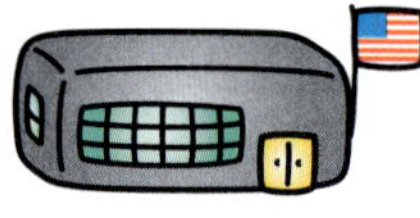
post office

store

library

fire station

Skills

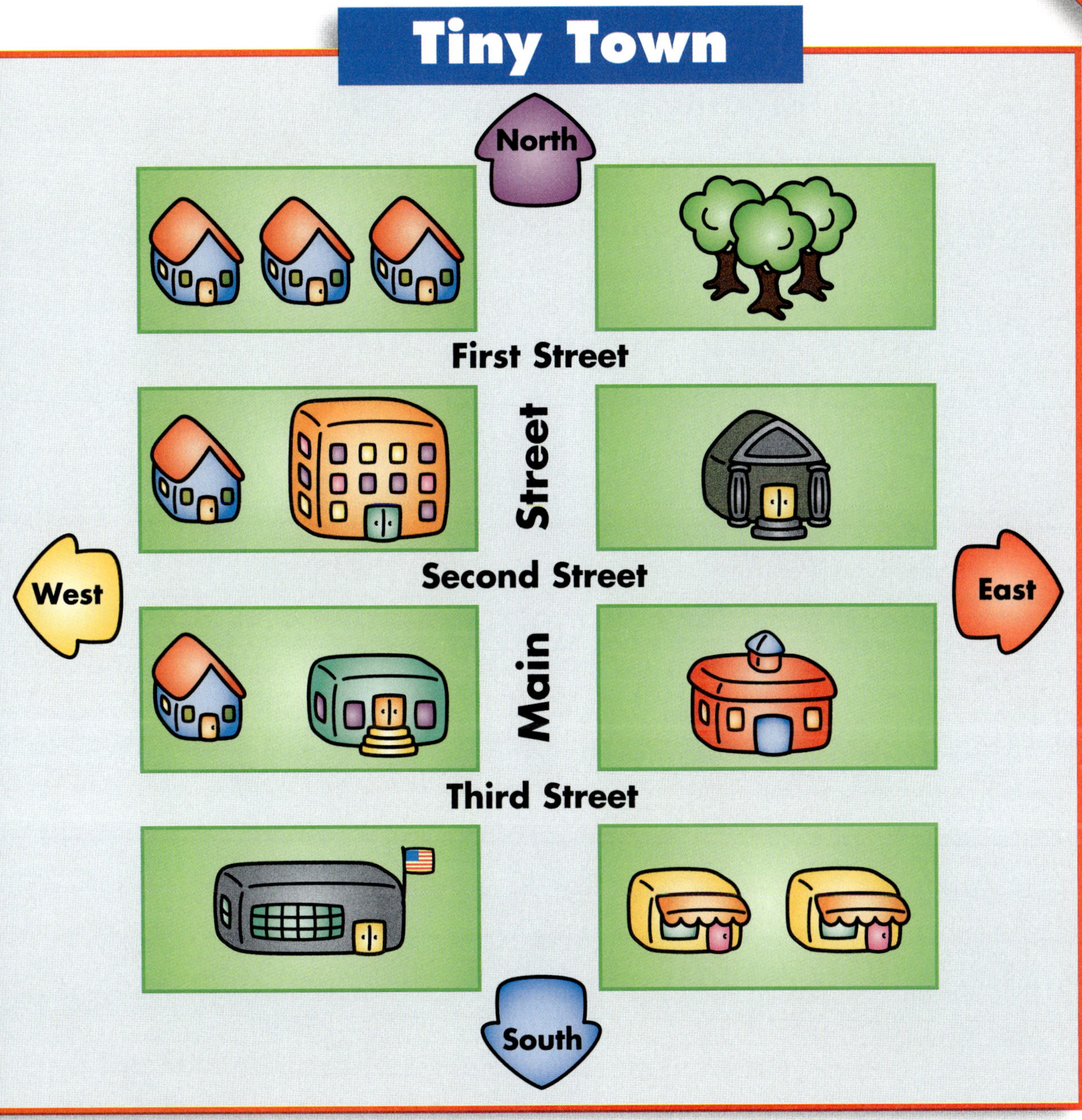

Think and Do

In which direction would a mail carrier go to get from the post office to the apartments?

LESSON

A Community Changes

My community has changed a lot. My dad told me it changed when a college was built here. He showed me pictures. I put the pictures into a book. I am taking the book to school for Show and Tell.

A lot of workers came to build the college. First they cleared the land. Then they started building.

After the college was built, many people moved here. These people needed houses. They needed stores to buy food and clothes. They needed more roads. The community grew.

My dad says the changes have been good for our community. We like having the college close by. Someday I might go there.

Biography

Frank Lloyd Wright was a famous architect. He used ideas from nature in his buildings. You can see some of his work at Florida Southern College in Lakeland, Florida.

What Do You Know?

1. Name three changes that happened in the community.
2. What changes have happened in your community?

Solving Problems

Change and People

People move for many reasons. They may move to find a new job or to live in a bigger house.

More people are moving to Kim's community. More houses are being built near the school. The school is small.

- How will these changes affect Kim?
- How will these changes affect the school?

Show Your Ideas

- Kim's school will change. Draw a picture to show what might happen.
- More cars will be on the streets. How could the streets be kept safe?

Brainstorm

LESSON

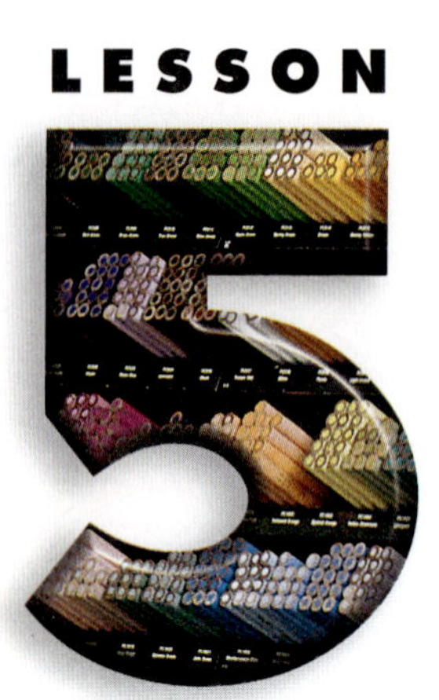

Trading Goods and Services

We use money to buy goods and services. **Goods** are things people make or grow to sell or trade. People work to earn the money they need. Some children do jobs at home. Look at Brandon's list. What goods and services is he buying?

What service is being done in this shop?

My Shopping List
markers
paints
baseball bat
Get bike fixed.
dog leash
dog food

What goods can be found in these stores?

What Do You Know?

1. How do people earn money?
2. How do you spend your money?

Chart and Graph Skills

Read a Table

A **table** lists things in groups. This table shows who sells goods and who gives services.

1. Which side of the table shows people who sell goods? Which side shows people who give services?

2. Find the bus driver. Does the bus driver sell goods or give a service?

3. Who sells goods that people eat?

Think and Do

Think of two more workers for this table. Who could go on the goods side? Who could go on the services side?

Skills

Goods and Services

People Who Sell Goods	People Who Give Services
 **bookseller**	 **firefighter**
 **butcher**	 **dentist**
 **baker**	 **bus driver**

LESSON

Getting from Here to There

There are many ways to move from place to place. The ways people, goods, and ideas travel change over time. These are some ways they have traveled on land.

US10c 200 Years of Postal Service

People, goods, and ideas don't always travel on land. They travel on water, too.

Sometimes people, goods, and ideas travel in the air. Planes are faster than ships, trucks, and trains.

Charles Lindbergh

Biography

Ellen Ochoa is an astronaut. Dr. Ochoa has been on several space flights. On one flight she helped take goods to the International Space Station.

What Do You Know?

1. Name three ways people, goods, and ideas travel.
2. How do people, goods, and ideas travel in your community?

Friends in the Community

A class at Hillside Elementary School in Wisconsin has made some special friends. Their teacher started a program called Forever Friends. The children visit elders who live in the community. Everyone chooses a special friend.

United States

Brookfield, Wisconsin

Sometimes the elders visit the school. Then the friends read and write stories together.

They go on field trips, too. They have been to the fire station and the zoo.

The children and elders like being together. "It's great fun to be with the kids and hear what they have to say," said Mrs. O'Neill. "Just going places together is a lot of fun!"

Building Citizenship

What Can You Do?

- Find out about a place where elders live in your community. Write letters to them.
- Invite an elder friend to visit your school and share a story.

Visit the Internet at http://www.hbschool.com for additional resources.

Picture Summary

Look at the picture. It will help you remember what you learned.

Talk About the Main Ideas

1. Different people and groups live in a community.
2. Community leaders help people get along.
3. Communities sometimes change.
4. People work to earn money to buy goods and services.
5. People and goods move in many different ways.

Solve a Problem What are some problems this community has? Tell how community leaders might help solve the problems.

ART LEAGUE
BOOKS USED
BROWN LAW OFFICE
IRA'S
OFFICE SUPPLY
BEAUTIQUE MEN WOMEN
TAWANA'S HAIR CARE
DONALD & SONS
LOCKSMITH · KEYS
OPEN
W
WANG ♥ 24 HOUR ♥ GROCERY MARKET
SALAD BAR HERE
POST
ACE DELIVERY
ONE WAY
6th Ave. W. 22nd
ONE WAY
STOP
WALK
TOWN
MAYOR HAWTHORNE SPEAKS AT CITY HALL
TAXI
TAXI
RACHEL'S HOME FURNISHINGS
CITY GARBAGE
YMCA FUND DRIVE
CATS

Use Vocabulary

Which word does not belong in each box? Tell why.

1. **leader**
   mayor
   dancer
   principal

2. **goods**
   foods
   clothes
   rain

3. **services**
   fight fires
   play ball
   cut hair

4. **city**
   barns
   stores
   homes

5. **neighborhood**
   houses
   schools
   whales

Check Understanding

1. How are all communities the same?
2. Tell what two service workers do.
3. Name three ways a community can change.
4. How do people, goods, and ideas travel?

Think Critically

What are some of the problems that might happen when too many cars and buses are on the road?

Apply Skills

Find Directions on a Map

Use the map to find places in the community.

1. What is north of City Hall?
2. What building is to the south of the school?
3. In what direction would you go to get from the hospital to the school?

Apply Skills

Do It Yourself

Make a table. Show ways people traveled long ago and today. Look on pages 106–109 for ideas. Look at other books, too.

1. Fold a sheet of paper in half.
2. Write Then on one half and Now on the other half.
3. Draw ways to travel then and now.
4. Give your table a title.

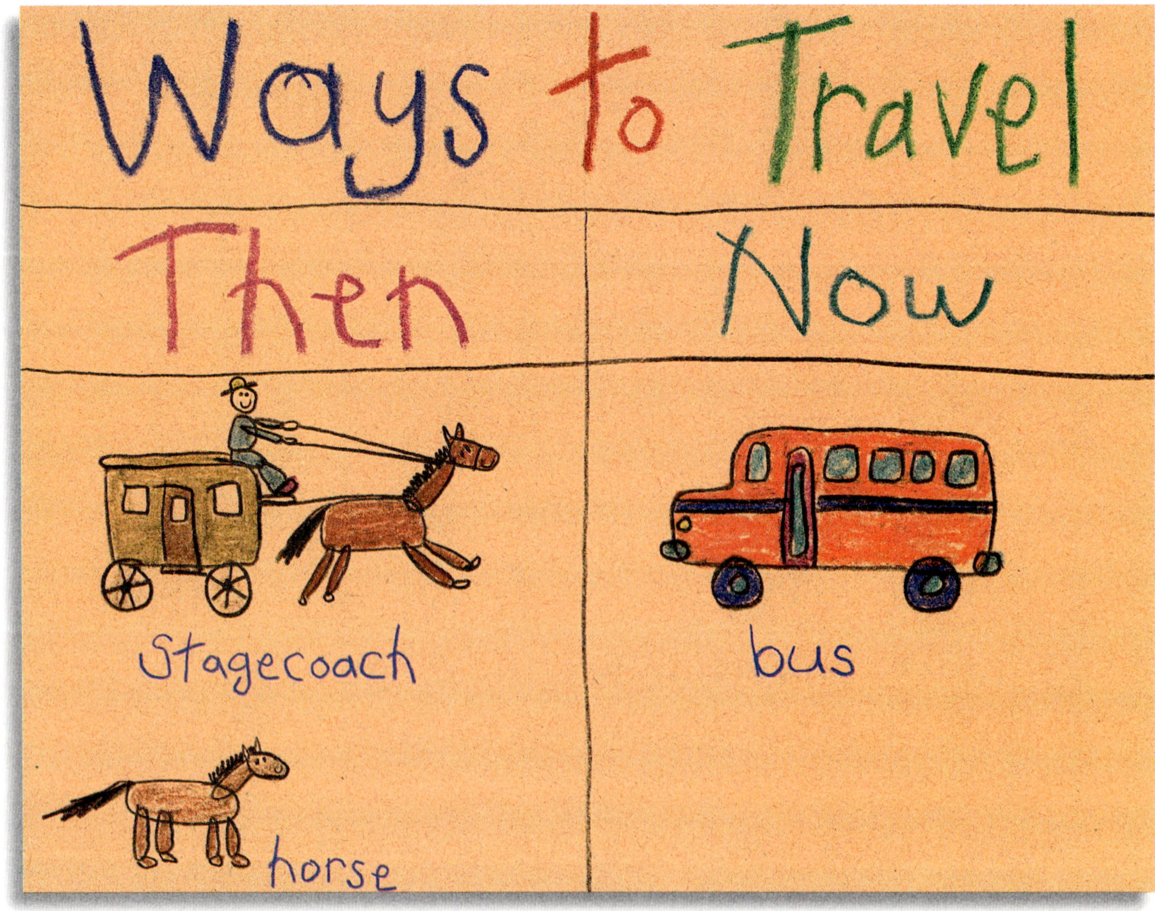

Unit Activity

Make a Riddle Game

 Fold a sheet of paper in half to make each riddle card.

 On the inside, draw a community building or worker.

 On the outside, write a riddle about the picture.

 Play a riddle game with the cards.

Visit the Internet at http://www.hbschool.com for additional resources.

Read More About It

Pelle's New Suit by Elsa Beskow. Floris. Many workers help make Pelle's new suit.

The Big Green Pocketbook by Candice Ransom. HarperCollins. A girl fills her pocketbook with interesting things from a trip around town.

Taking a Walk/Caminando by Rebecca Emberley. Little, Brown. Walk through a neighborhood and learn the English and Spanish names of things.

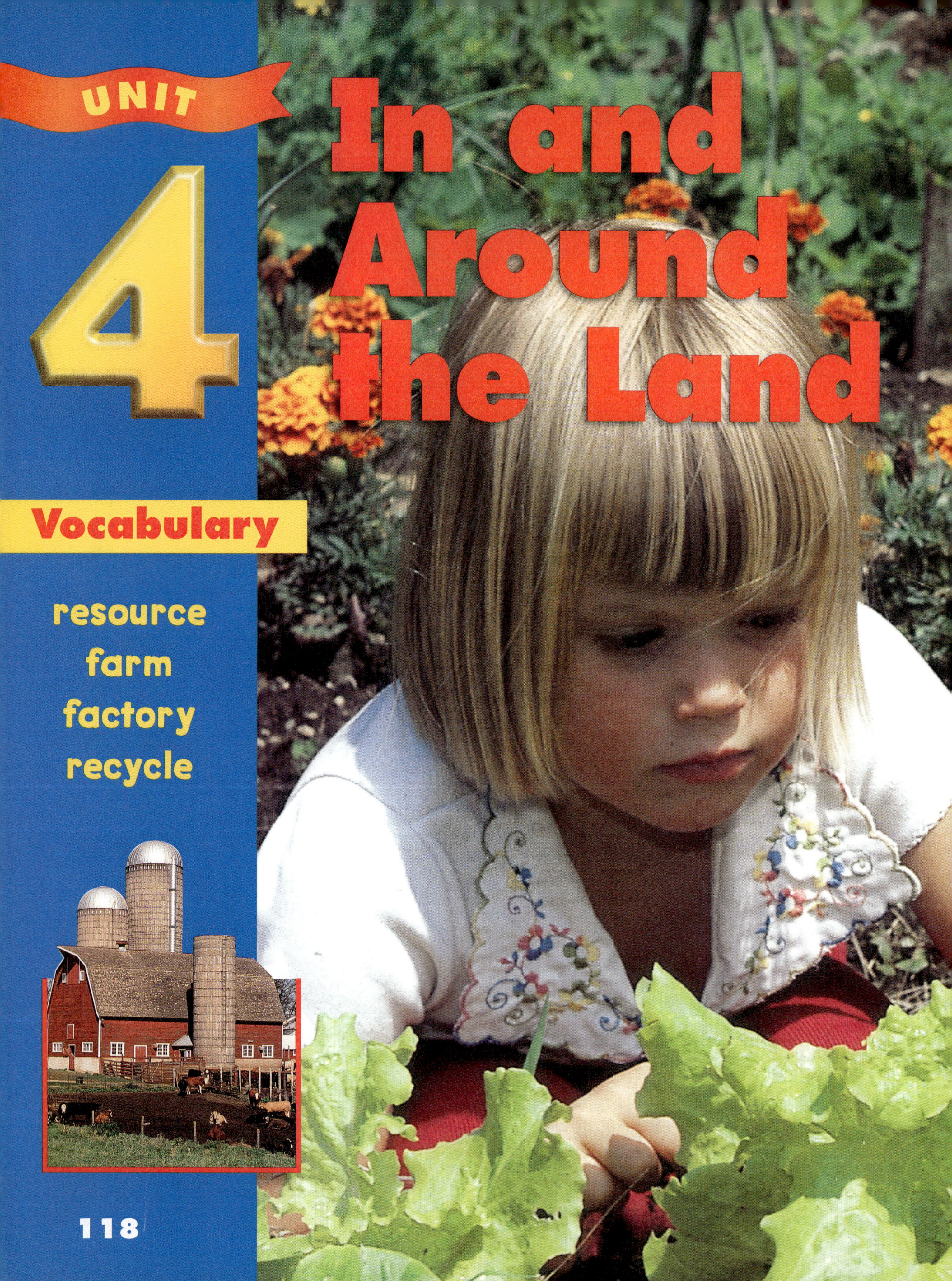

UNIT 4

In and Around the Land

Vocabulary

resource
farm
factory
recycle

resource

farm

factory
recycle

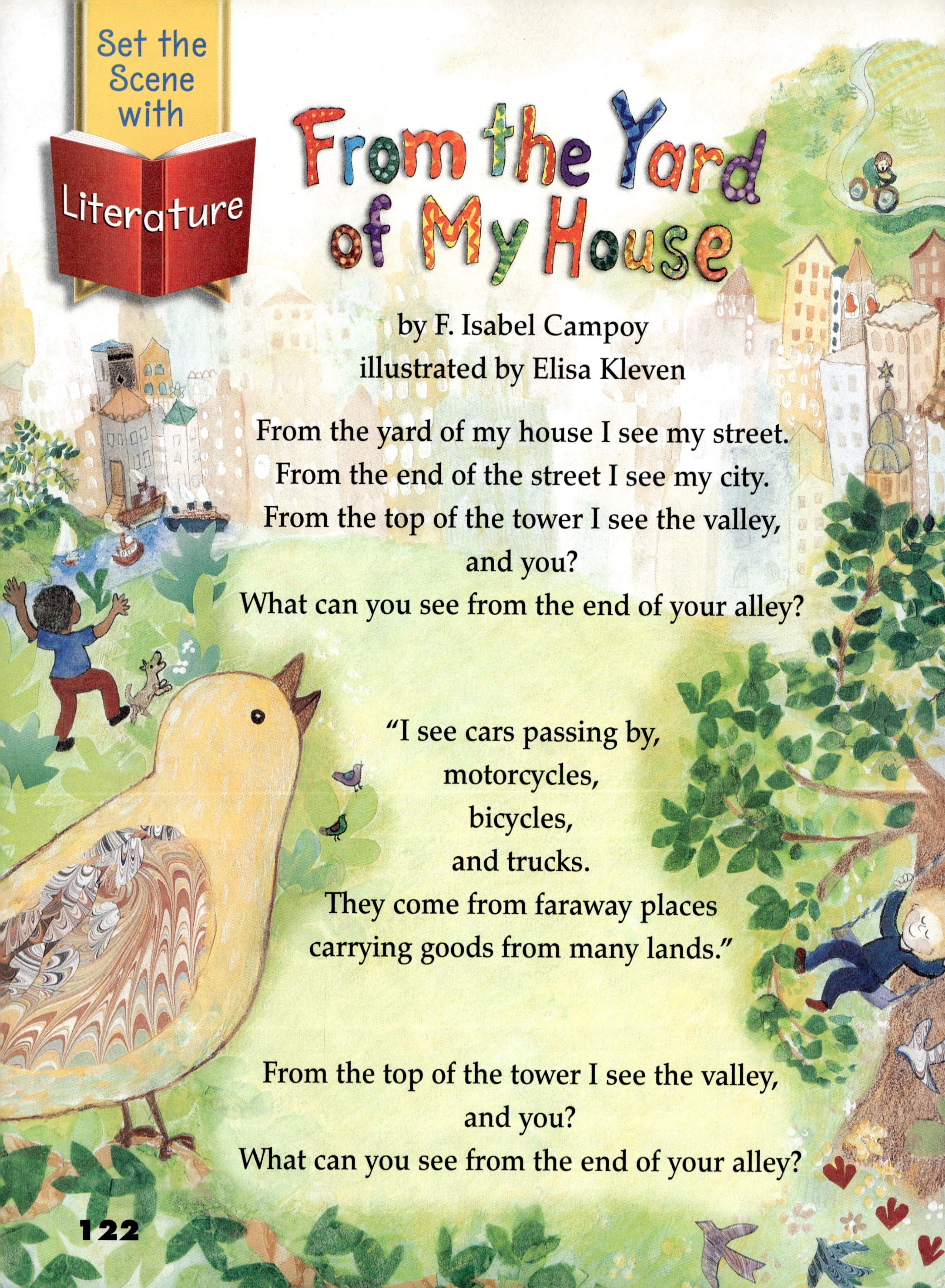

From the Yard of My House

by F. Isabel Campoy
illustrated by Elisa Kleven

From the yard of my house I see my street.
From the end of the street I see my city.
From the top of the tower I see the valley,
and you?
What can you see from the end of your alley?

"I see cars passing by,
motorcycles,
bicycles,
and trucks.
They come from faraway places
carrying goods from many lands."

From the top of the tower I see the valley,
and you?
What can you see from the end of your alley?

LESSON 1

Land and Water

This drawing shows different kinds of land and water. Read the picture dictionary on the next page to find out about each one.

A **hill** is land that rises up high but not as high as a mountain.

A **lake** is a body of water that has land around it.

A **mountain** is the highest kind of land.

An **ocean** is the largest body of water, and its water is salty.

A **plain** is land that is mostly flat.

A **river** is a long body of water that flows through the land.

What Do You Know?

What kinds of land and water are near your community?

Find Land and Water on a Map

This map shows land and water. It uses pictures and colors to show where things are.

1. Look at the map key. What pictures and colors do you see?
2. Find the river and the lake. How are they the same?

Map Key

plains

mountains

picnic area

lake

woods

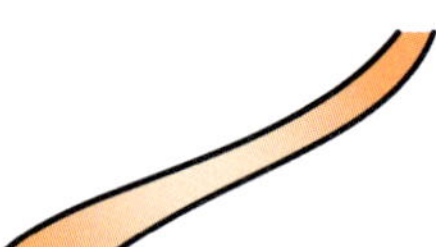

hiking trail

river

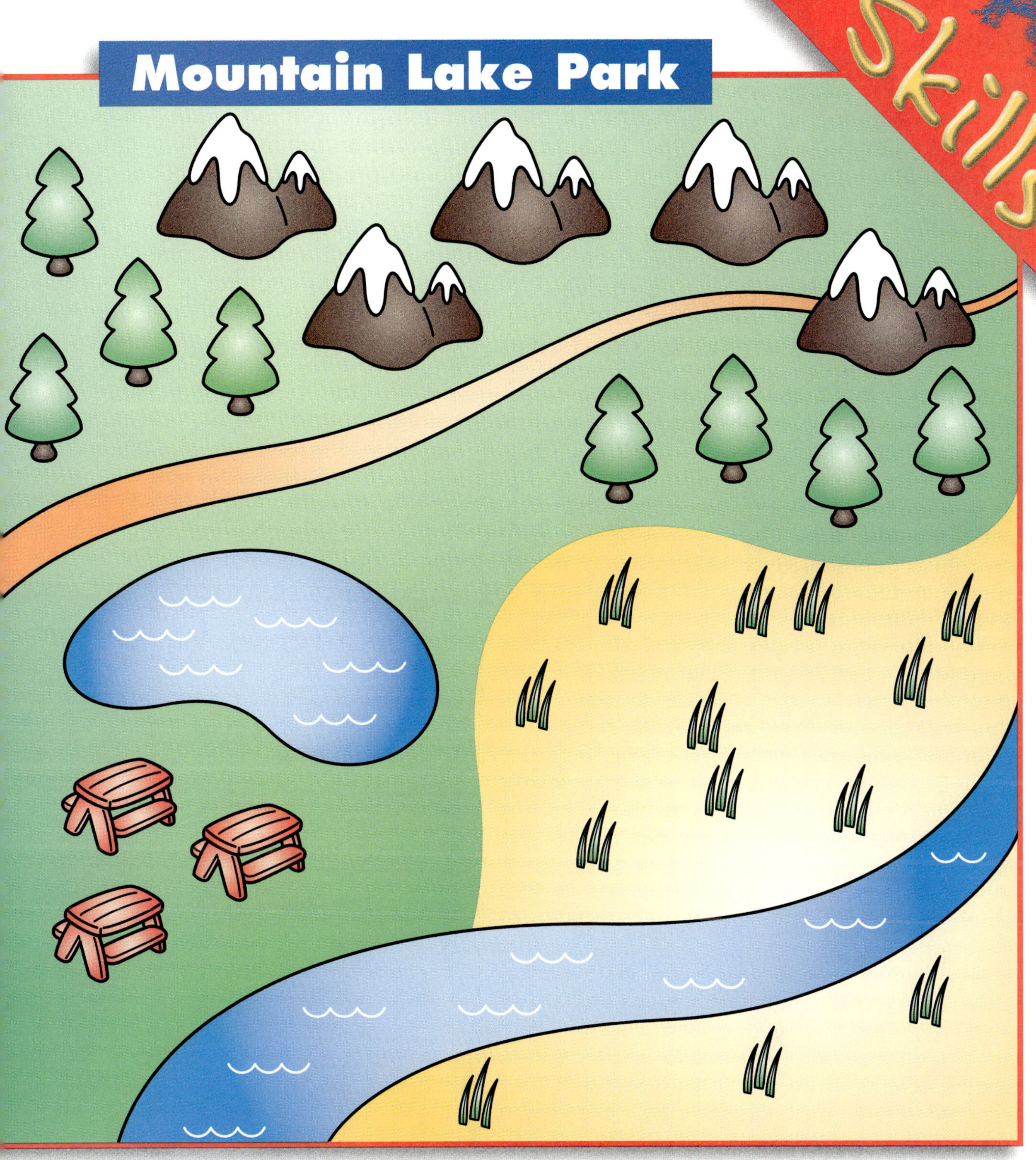

Think and Do

Look at the map. What is between the hiking trail and the picnic tables?

LESSON 2

Our Treasured Resources

A **resource** is something people use to meet their needs. Trees, soil, water, oil, and gas are resources. Read this report to find out about our resources.

Our Resources

Trees are an important resource. Many trees grow in a **forest**. Wood and food come from trees. Wood is used to make buildings and furniture. Two foods that grow on trees are apples and walnuts.

Oil and gas are resources. They come from under the ground. People use oil and gas to heat their homes and cook their food. Some oil is made into gasoline. Cars need oil and gasoline to run.

Biography

In 1908 Henry Ford sold his first Model T cars. His cars cost less than other cars. Soon many people owned cars. This brought changes to many communities. In 1921 the first drive-in restaurant opened in Dallas, Texas. Servers brought the food out to people in their cars.

Soil is another resource. Soil is the ground trees and other plants must grow in.

Soil is very important to farms. A **farm** is land that is used to grow plants and raise animals. The plants and animals help us meet our needs for food and clothing.

Biography

Marjory Stoneman Douglas helped to save the Florida Everglades. The Everglades is a low, wet land with tall grass. Ms. Douglas loved this land. She wrote many books about it. Today the Florida Everglades is a National Park.

Water is a resource, too. People must have water to live. Water comes from lakes, rivers, and oceans.

Water is important for drinking. Water also gives us food. Fish come from lakes, rivers, and oceans.

What Do You Know?

1. Why are trees an important resource?
2. What resources do you use?

LESSON 3

People Change the Land

Our class is learning about ways people change the land. One way they do this is by building dams. Dams hold back water. I brought a picture of a dam I built. It held back the water so I could sail my boat.

I also brought a picture of a real dam. I visited the Hoover Dam with my family. A worker told us what it was like there long ago. Communities near the river were being flooded. They needed a dam to hold back the water.

Many people worked for a long time to build the dam. Now floods are not a problem.

Hoover Dam helps many communities. Some of the water goes into machines to make electricity. Some water goes to farms and to homes.

History

In the hills of South Dakota, workers carved the faces of American Presidents in the stone. The Presidents shown are George Washington, Thomas Jefferson, Theodore Roosevelt, and Abraham Lincoln.

The worker told us there was no lake there before the dam was built. The water that the dam held back made Lake Mead. My family and I swam in the lake.

The worker gave me some things for my class. Now everyone wants to visit Hoover Dam!

What Do You Know?

1. What is one way people change the land?
2. How have people changed the land where you live?

What Kind of House?

Sometimes people find ways to live on the land without changing it. They build houses that fit the land where they live. Talk about why people built these houses the way they did.

What Would You Do?

- Imagine that you live in a place where it rains a lot. The water gets very deep. There are many trees.
- How would you build a house in this place? Draw a picture of it.
- Write some sentences to tell how you made your choice.

LESSON

The Cheese Factory

Do you know what resources are used to make cheese? Mrs. Karl's class visited a factory to find out. A **factory** is a place where something is made.

Cheese

We like it on sandwiches,
tacos, and crackers.

We spread it and slice it
and grate it.

There's nothing quite like it
for after-school snackers.

Oh dear. It's all gone.
Guess I ate it!

1 This is the way cheese begins. First, dairy farmers raise the cows that give milk.

2 Next, trucks take milk from the dairy farm to the cheese factory. There the milk is made into cheese.

To make the cheese, the milk is heated and cooled.

3

4

The liquid part is drained away. The solid part is pressed into blocks.

5

The blocks are salted and dipped in wax.

6

When the cheese is ready, trucks carry the cheese to stores.

7

Then the cheese is cut into smaller pieces.

What Do You Know?

1. Where do cheese factories get their milk?
2. What surprised you about how cheese is made?

Read a Pictograph

After the field trip, Mrs. Karl's class talked about the things made from milk. Mrs. Karl made a pictograph. A **pictograph** uses pictures to show how many there are of something. This is how to read one.

1. What is the title of this pictograph?
2. Find the key. What does each picture of a face stand for?
3. Find and name the foods on the pictograph.
4. How many faces are next to the milk? How many children had milk?

Skills

Dairy Foods We Ate

Food	Children

Key

 = 1 child

Think and Do

- Which dairy food was eaten by the most children?
- How many more children ate cheese than yogurt?

LESSON

Saving Our Resources

It is our responsibility to save Earth's resources. Mr. Smith's class made a flyer about how to save resources.

Reduce

- Turn off the water while you brush your teeth.
- Walk or ride your bike instead of having someone drive you.
- Shut off the lights when you leave the room. That saves electricity.

Reuse

You can reuse many things.

- Use plastic bags and glass bottles again.
- Make a pencil holder from a can.
- Grow plants in a plastic bottle.

Recycle

- Used plastic bags, paper, cans, and glass can be recycled.
- Find a place to collect the things you can recycle.
- Put them out to be picked up or take them to a recycling center.

What Do You Know?

1. Why is it our responsibility to recycle things?
2. What things do you reduce, reuse, or recycle?

Critical Thinking Skills

Find Out What People Think

A first-grade class is planning a picnic. The children cannot decide whether to take paper or plastic cups and plates. They decide to find out what everyone thinks.

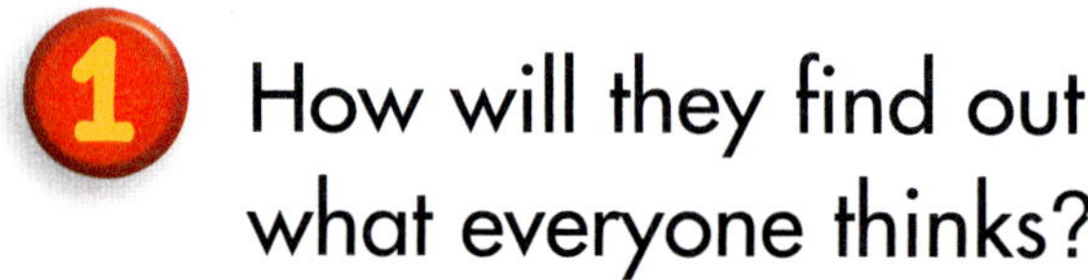

1. How will they find out what everyone thinks?
2. What are they asking?
3. How can they use what they find out?

Think and Do

What would you take on the picnic? Answer the questions on page 147.

What Would You Take?

If you were planning a picnic, what would you take?

Circle one kind of plate and one kind of cup.

1. Plates: plastic paper other

Reason ______________________

2. Cups: plastic paper other

Reason ______________________

How Does Your Garden Grow?

Berkeley, California

Hello, my name is Neanna. I go to Le Conte Elementary School in Berkeley, California.

My school has a garden. In our garden we grow tomatoes, sunflowers, corn and other plants. Everyone helps take care of the garden.

We work in groups to use all the parts of the plants. One group pops corn seeds to make popcorn. One group cooks vegetable soup. We even make dolls from cornstalks and roots!

We put seeds in small packs and sell them. We use the money to buy things for the garden.

What Can You Do?

- List ways a garden might help people in a community.
- Read books about healthful foods. What might you grow in a garden where you live?

Visit the Internet at http://www.hbschool.com for additional resources.

Picture Summary

Follow the pictures. They will help you remember what you learned.

Talk About the Main Ideas

1. There are different kinds of land and water.
2. Resources come from land and water.
3. People change the land.
4. Factories use resources to make things we need.
5. People help save resources.

Draw Me I am a resource that lives in a brook. If you want to catch me, you need a sharp hook. People cook me and serve me on a dish. Do you know what I am? I'm just a little _____!

FACTORY
MARKET
Apple Juice $1.29
SALE
GLASS ONLY

Use Vocabulary

Which word goes with each box?

factory farm resource recycle

1. something people use that comes from the earth
2. place where people raise plants and animals for food and clothing
3. place where things are made that people want to buy
4. make something old into something new

Check Understanding

1. Tell about three kinds of land.
2. Name two resources that come from the land. How do people use each of them?
3. How do people change the land?
4. How do people work together to save resources?

Think Critically

How can saving the Earth's resources help us?

Apply Skills

Read a Pictograph

Use the pictograph to answer the questions.

1. Which place do most of the children like best?
2. How many children chose the mountains?
3. More children chose the farm than the city. How many more chose the farm?

Do It Yourself

Make your own pictograph. Draw other places to go in your community. Find out which place children like best.

Apply Skills

Find Land and Water on a Map

Draw a map to show what you see in the photograph. Make a map key to show what the land and water look like on the map.

Find Out What People Think

Would your classmates like to work in a cheese factory? You can find out by asking questions.

1. Write your questions on some sheets of paper.
2. Give the papers to your classmates.
3. Read what people think.

Unit Activity

Recycling Station

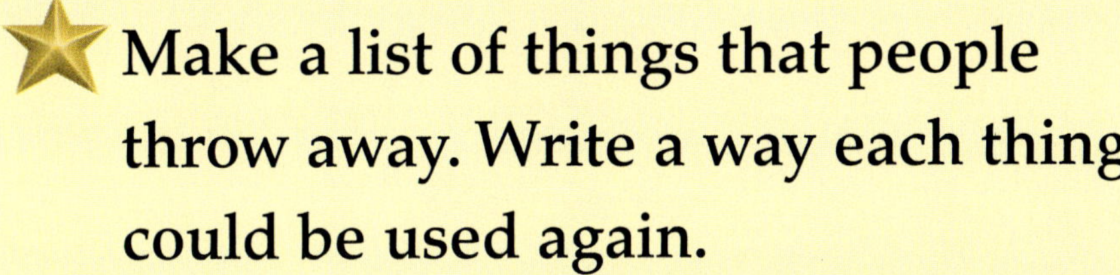

- Make a list of things that people throw away. Write a way each thing could be used again.

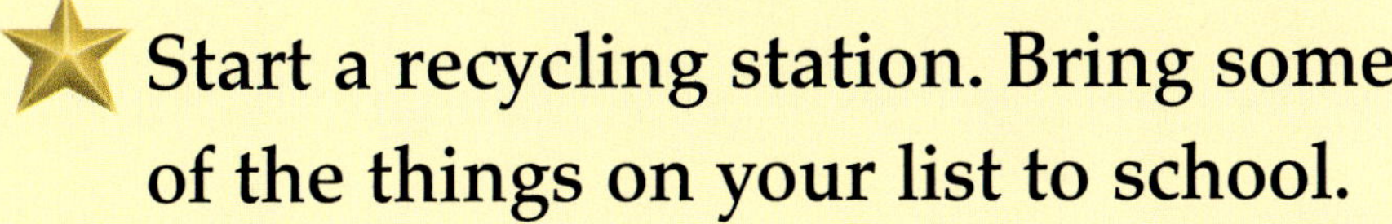

- Start a recycling station. Bring some of the things on your list to school.

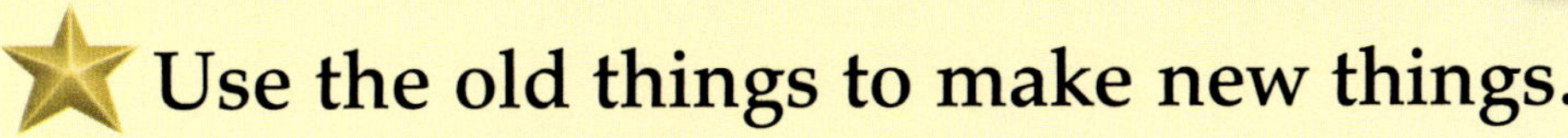

- Use the old things to make new things.

Visit the Internet at http://www.hbschool.com for additional resources.

Read More About It

The Diggers by Margaret Wise Brown. Hyperion. Workers dig a train tunnel through a mountain.

Where the Forest Meets the Sea by Jeannie Baker. Greenwillow. A boy sees many beautiful things when he visits a rain forest with his father.

Water by Carme Solé Vendrell and J. M. Parramón. Barron's. Two children find out many ways that water is used.

UNIT 5

My Country, My Heroes

Vocabulary

flag
country
state
history
President
law

Unit 5 Preview

flag

country

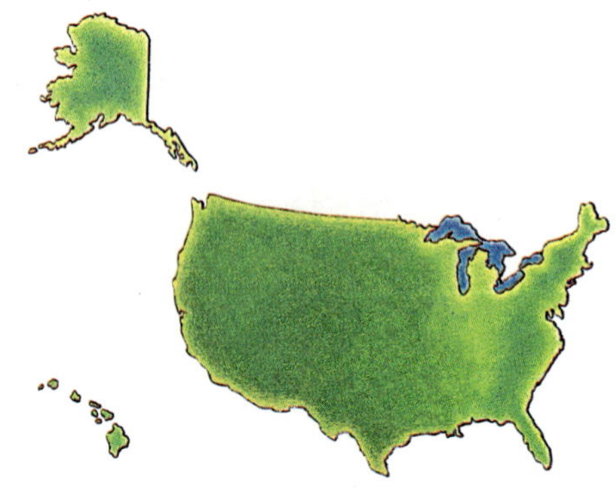

state

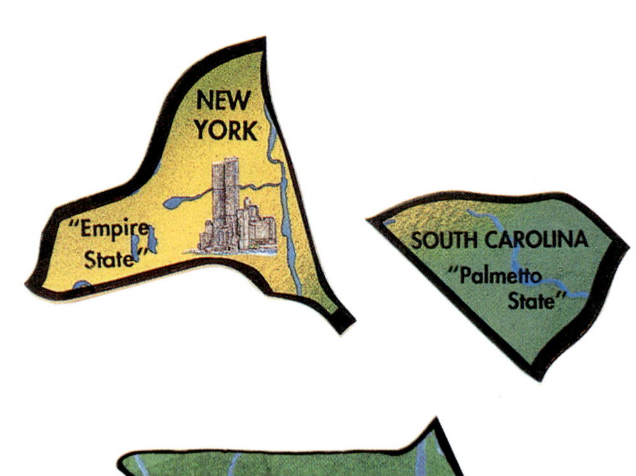

President

history

law

Set the Scene with
Literature

The Pledge of Allegiance

illustrated by Barbara Maslen

I pledge allegiance
to the **flag** of the
United States
of America,
and to the Republic
for which it stands,
one Nation
under God,
indivisible,
with liberty
and justice
for all.

LESSON 1

Sharing the Land

South Carolina's Flag

The puzzle below is a map of our country. A **country** is a land and the people who live in that land. Our country is the United States of America. The United States of America is very big. Many Americans share our country.

A **state** is one part of our country. The United States has 50 states. Each state has its own name.

This is another map of our country. It shows the countries that are our neighbors. Mexico is our neighbor to the south. Canada is our neighbor to the north.

This map also shows two oceans. The Atlantic Ocean is to the east of our country. The Pacific Ocean is to the west.

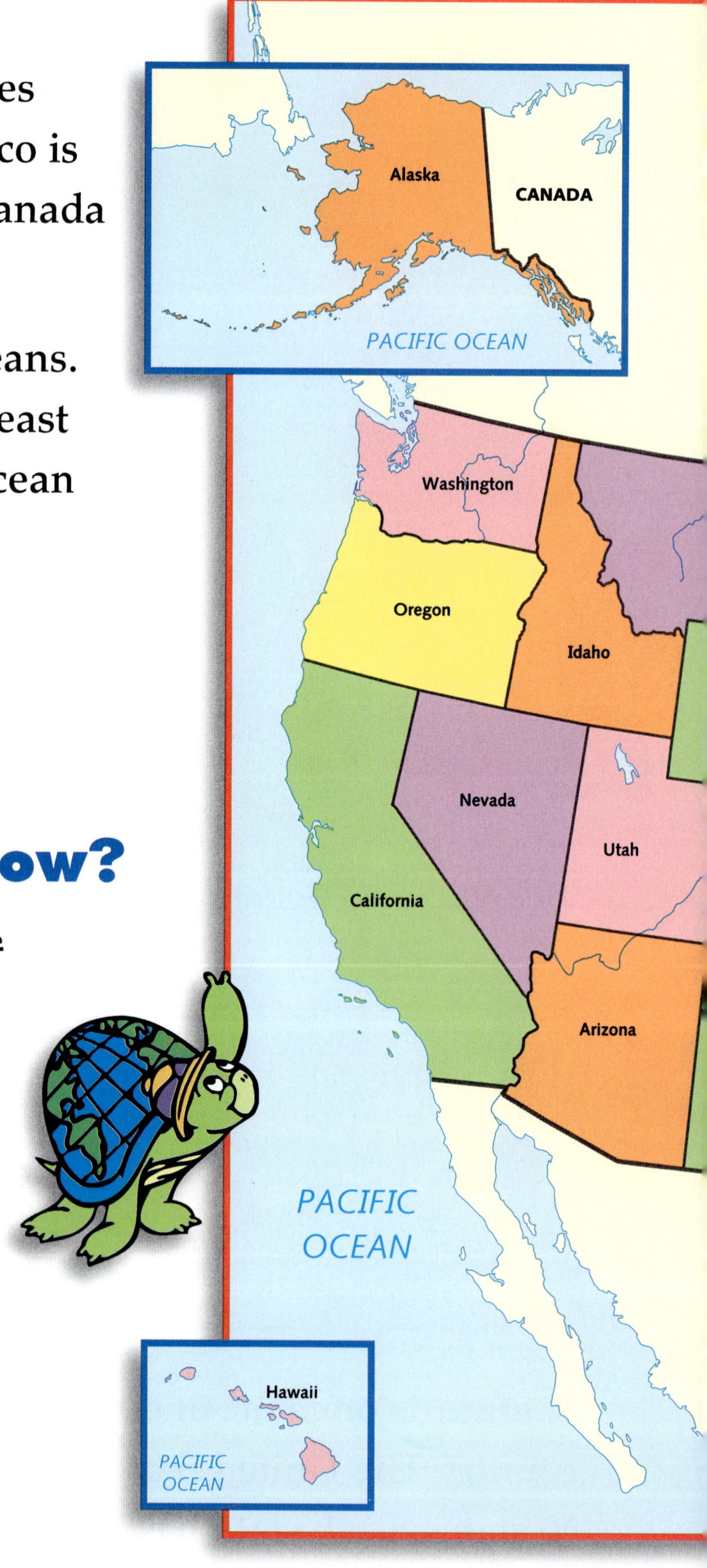

What Do You Know?

1. What is the name of our country?
2. Which states are your neighbors?

United States of America

LESSON

Two Groups of People Meet

This is the story of how two groups of people first met long, long ago. We know what happened because a ship's captain wrote a log. His name was Christopher Columbus. Read about his long trip across the ocean.

Friday, August 3, 1492

Columbus and his crew sailed away from Spain. They sailed on three ships called the Niña, the Pinta, and the Santa María.

Sunday, September 9, 1492

Columbus and his crew were far from home. They had not seen land for a long time.

Thursday, October 11, 1492

Columbus saw lights from far away. At last the ships were near land.

Friday, October 12, 1492

Columbus and his crew landed on the beach of an island. They met the friendly people who lived there.

Columbus called the people he met Indians. The Indians had never seen anyone like Columbus before. His clothes and his words were strange to them.

Columbus and the Indians traded many things. The Indians gave Columbus foods he had never tasted before.

Columbus took corn, peanuts, sweet potatoes, and tomatoes back to Spain.

One year later he came back. He brought horses, pigs, goats, and sheep for the Indians.

Columbus told people about the islands he had found. Many more people crossed the ocean. Soon things changed for everyone.

What Do You Know?

1. How do we know what happened to Christopher Columbus?
2. Why do you think people today celebrate Columbus Day?

Chart and Graph Skills

Read a Calendar

Columbus used a calendar on his trip. A **calendar** shows what time of year it is. This calendar shows October. How many days are in October?

October

Sunday	Monday	Tuesday	Wednesday	Thursday	Friday	Saturday
	1	2 Rosh Hashanah	3	4 Children's Day	5	6
7	8	9	10 Health and Sports Day in Japan	11	12 Columbus Day	13
14	15	16 Dictionary Day	17	18	19	20
21	22	23	24	25	26	27
28 Daylight Savings Time Ends	29	30	31			

October is a fall month. Fall is one part of the year called a **season**. The other seasons are winter, spring, and summer.

Skills

1. Read page 167. Then find Columbus Day on the calendar. Why do you think Columbus Day is October 12?

2. Find October 4th on the calendar. What day of the week is it? On this day we remember children all over the world.

3. Noah Webster wrote the first American dictionary. Dictionary Day is his birthday. On what date is Dictionary Day?

Think and Do

Make a list of things you do at school for one week. Write the day on which you do each thing.

LESSON 3

Independence Day

In America, the Fourth of July is a special holiday. It is called Independence Day. That is our country's birthday.

We celebrate America's history on Independence Day. **History** is the story of our country's past.

The Declaration of Independence by John Trumbull

Long ago, part of America belonged to a country called England. The people had to follow England's rules.

On July 4, 1776, American leaders signed the Declaration of Independence. It told the King of England that Americans wanted to be free.

Geography

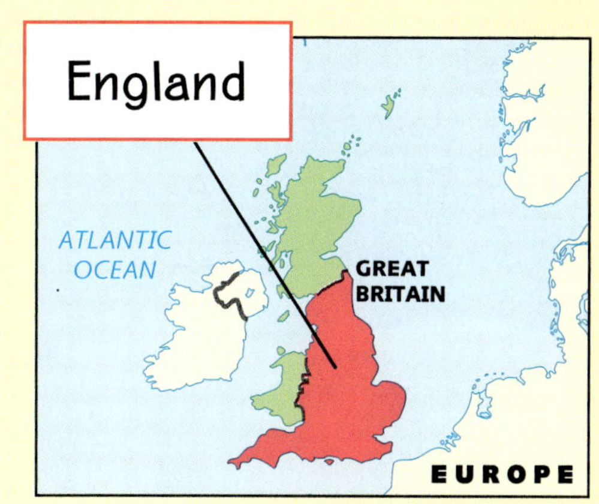

England is a country in Great Britain. Great Britain is a very large island. England has beautiful plains, hills, and mountains.

Americans fought a war to be free. General George Washington led the Americans against British soldiers. He helped the Americans win. Today all Americans have the right to be free.

Washington Crossing the Delaware by Emanuel Leutze

Washington was a **hero**. Americans chose him as the first President of the United States of America. He is called the Father of Our Country.

The **President** is the leader of our country. Washington's wife, Martha, was our country's first First Lady.

What Do You Know?

1. Why is the Fourth of July our country's birthday?
2. What other heroes do you know?

Make a Choice by Voting

Citizens choose their leaders by voting. **Citizens** have the right to vote because they are members of our country. A **vote** is a choice that gets counted. Voting is an important responsibility that citizens have. The person who gets the most votes wins. Here is how voting works.

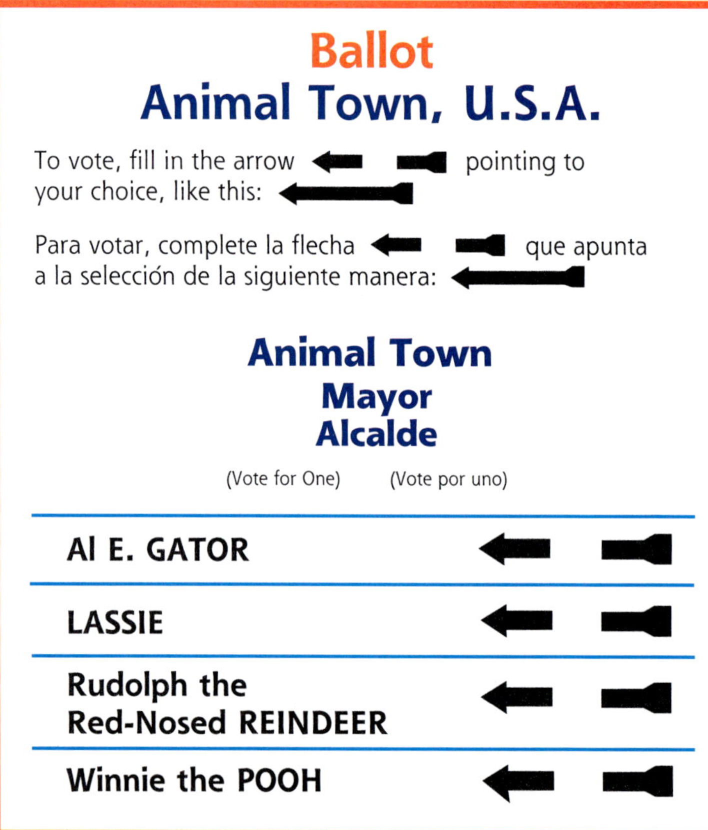

Ballot
Animal Town, U.S.A.

To vote, fill in the arrow pointing to your choice, like this:

Para votar, complete la flecha que apunta a la selección de la siguiente manera:

Animal Town
Mayor
Alcalde

(Vote for One) (Vote por uno)

Al E. GATOR

LASSIE

Rudolph the Red-Nosed REINDEER

Winnie the POOH

1 Imagine that Animal Town needs a new mayor. Four animals want the job.

Skills

2. Only one animal can be the new mayor. The citizens of Animal Town must choose by voting. The four names are put on a ballot. Each citizen may vote one time. The votes are kept secret.

3. After everyone votes, the votes are counted. The animal that gets the most votes wins. Voting is a fair way to choose leaders.

Think and Do

- Tell why citizens should learn about the people put on a ballot.
- Tell why voting is an important responsibility.

Laws Keep Us Safe

We need some laws. **Laws** are rules that everyone must follow.

Someone is going to get hurt.

Brainstorm

What problems do you see? Work with a group. Make a list of the problems.

What Would You Do?

Choose a way to show the class your ideas.

- Write how each problem can be solved.
- Act out your ways to solve the problems.
- Write some new laws.

America the Beautiful

by Katharine Lee Bates
illustrated by Neil Waldman

O beautiful for spacious skies,

For amber waves of grain,

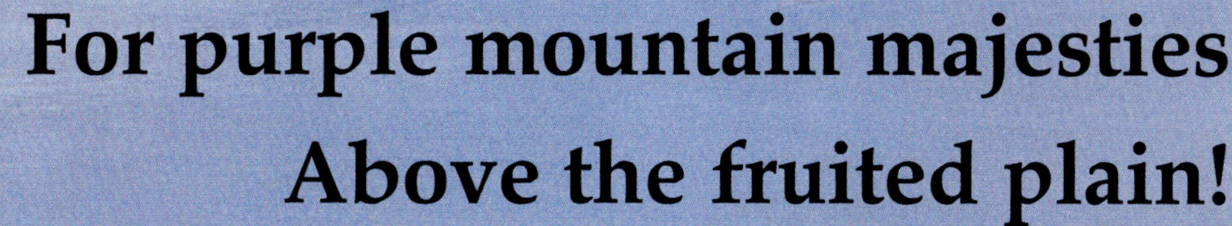

For purple mountain majesties
Above the fruited plain!

America! America!

God shed His grace on thee

And crown thy good
with brotherhood

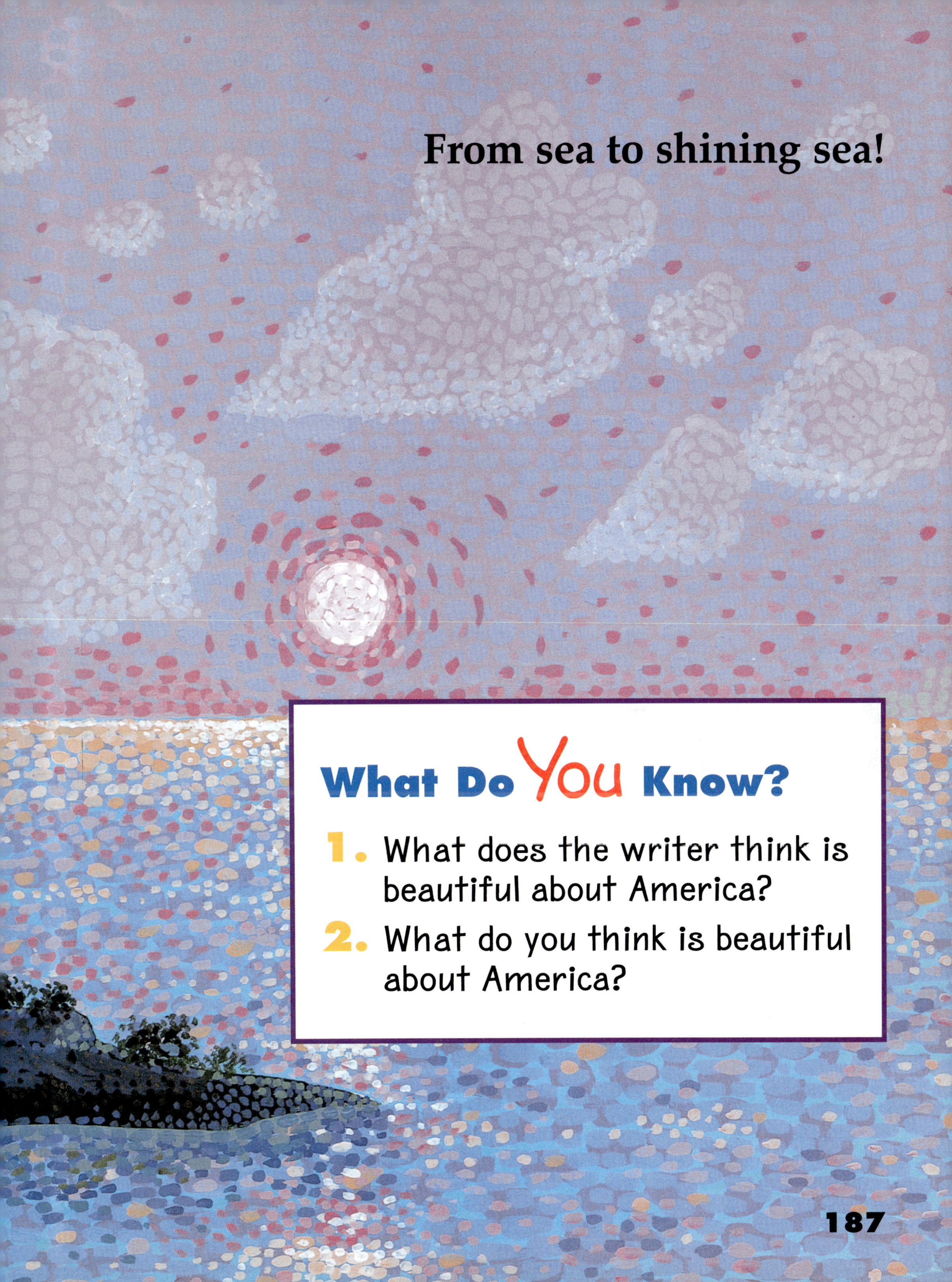

From sea to shining sea!

What Do You Know?

1. What does the writer think is beautiful about America?
2. What do you think is beautiful about America?

Chart and Graph Skills

Read a Diagram

The Statue of Liberty is our country's most famous statue. It stands for freedom. The lamp in Liberty's hand welcomes people who come to America. The picture on page 189 names the parts of the statue. It also shows you some things inside. This kind of picture is called a **diagram**.

1. Name the parts of the Statue of Liberty.

2. Find the crown. People can go inside the statue. How can they get up to the crown?

Think and Do

- If you were visiting the Statue of Liberty, how could this diagram help you?
- Find out the name of the island the statue stands on.

Skills

Statue of Liberty

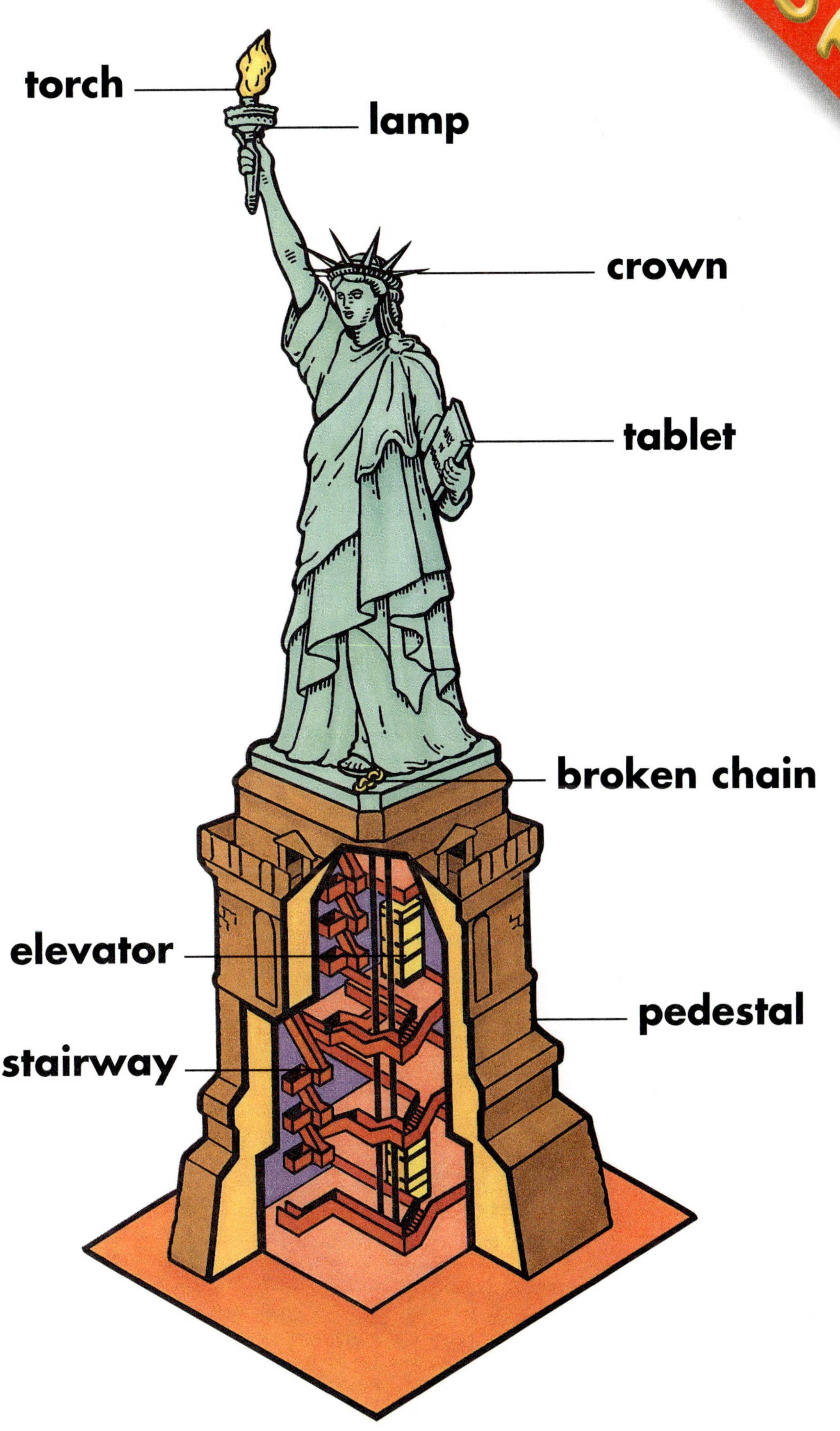

We Saved a Statue!

Some years ago, the Statue of Liberty needed to be fixed. Children helped earn the money to fix it.

Some first graders in Flint, Michigan, also found out that a statue of Benjamin Franklin was broken. Benjamin Franklin was an important leader in our country. He helped write the rules our country follows today. The first graders knew they could help fix the statue.

The children and their families saved 5,000 pennies. They mailed the pennies to Philadelphia, where the statue is. Other children sent pennies, too. Their pennies helped to fix the statue of Benjamin Franklin.

What Can You Do?

- Write to your mayor. Ask how statues in your community are cared for.
- Find out how you can help.

Picture Summary

Look at the pictures. They will help you remember what you learned.

Talk About the Main Ideas

1. The United States today has fifty states.
2. Long ago, Columbus led the way for new people to come to America.
3. Americans fought a war to be free, and our country began.
4. Americans are proud of their free and beautiful country.

Act It Out You and your friend are sailing to America. Tell why you want this country to be your new home.

history
state
country
law
President
flag

Use Vocabulary

Which word goes with each line?

1. United States, Mexico, Canada
2. Alaska, Ohio, Texas, Hawaii
3. fifty stars, thirteen stripes
4. Do not speed. Stop at red lights.
5. leader, George Washington
6. the story of our country's past

Check Understanding

1. How are a country and a state different?
2. What people were already living in America when Columbus landed there?
3. What foods did the Indians give Columbus? What did Columbus give the Indians?
4. Americans fought a war with England. Why?

Think Critically

Why is voting important to Americans?

Apply Skills

Make a Choice by Voting

Mrs. Lee's class wanted a class president. They wanted Jeff or Tamika for the job. Each child in the class voted. The table shows who won.

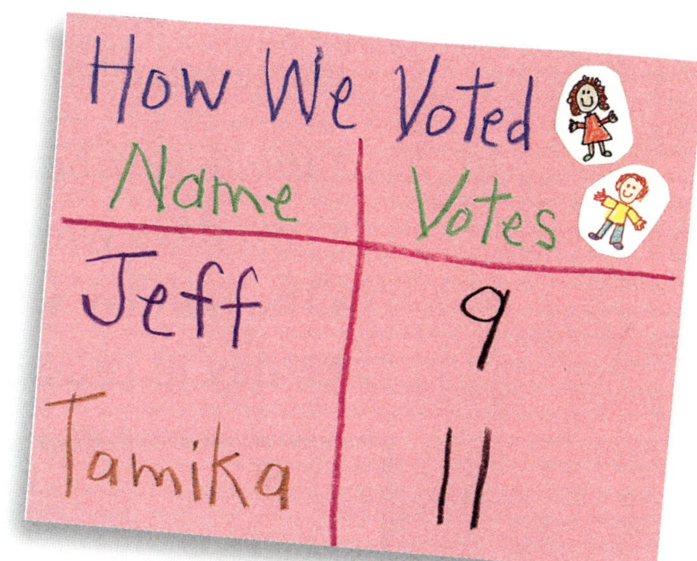

1. Who will be the class president? Why?
2. How many children voted for Jeff?
3. There are 20 children in the class. How many times did each child vote?

Do It Yourself

Write a question with two choices. Ask your classmates to vote. Write numbers to show the votes for each choice.

Apply Skills

Read a Calendar

Find these four things on the calendar.
Write what you find.

- the date when people vote
- two days when you do not go to school
- the holiday when families share a big meal
- a day to celebrate American soldiers

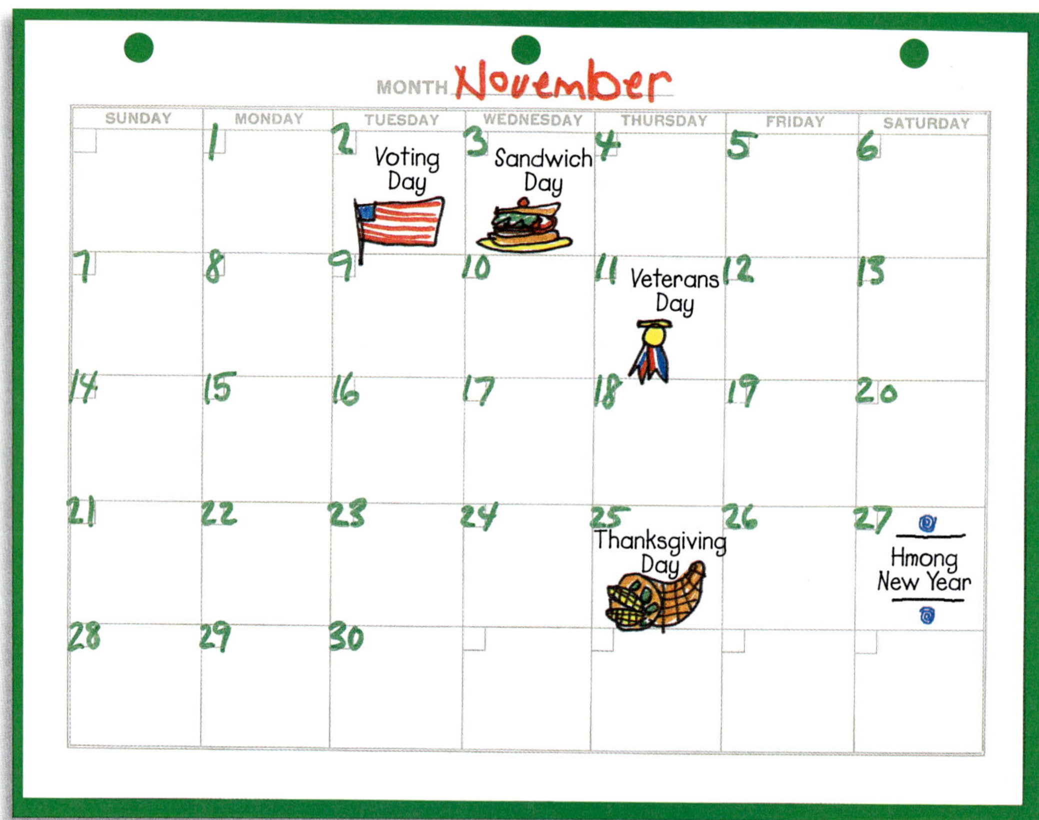

Make a Diagram

Draw a flag on a flagpole. Name the parts. Show where the flag and the pole are. Show where the stars and stripes are on the flag.

Unit Activity

Make a U.S.A. Flap Book

 Fold a sheet of paper in half.

 Cut three flaps. Write U.S.A. with one letter on each flap.

 Draw a picture about our country under each flap.

Visit the Internet at http://www.hbschool.com for additional resources.

Read More About It

Aunt Flossie's Hats (and Crab Cakes Later) by Elizabeth Fitzgerald Howard. Clarion. Two girls learn about history by listening to their Aunt's stories.

Buttons for General Washington by Peter and Connie Roop. Carolrhoda. Find out how General Washington's coat buttons helped him win a war.

Sam the Minuteman by Nathaniel Benchley. HarperCollins. A boy named Sam sees British soldiers march into his town.

UNIT

6

My World Near and Far

Vocabulary

world
globe
continent
language

ATLANTIC

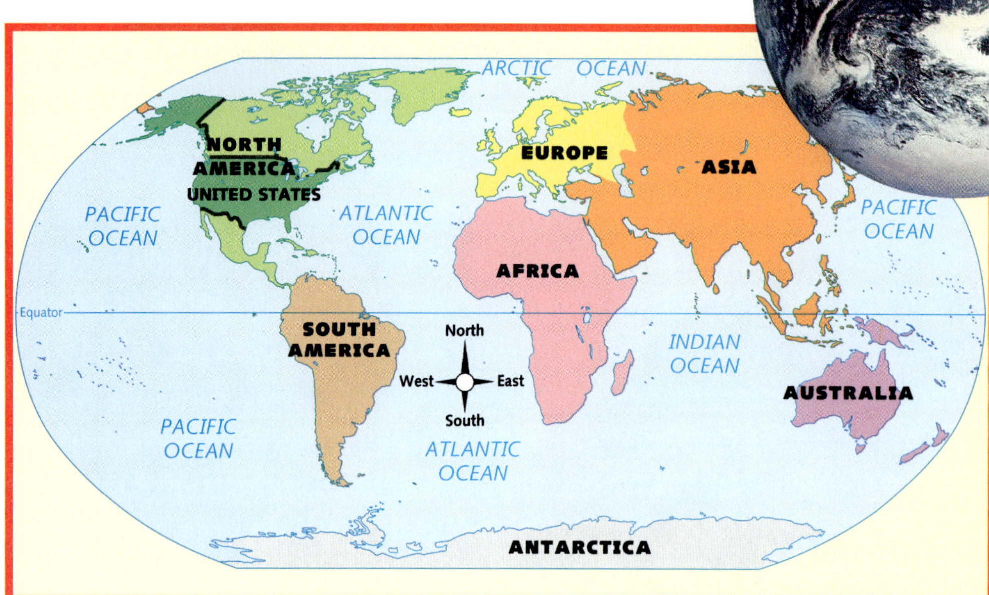

globe

continent

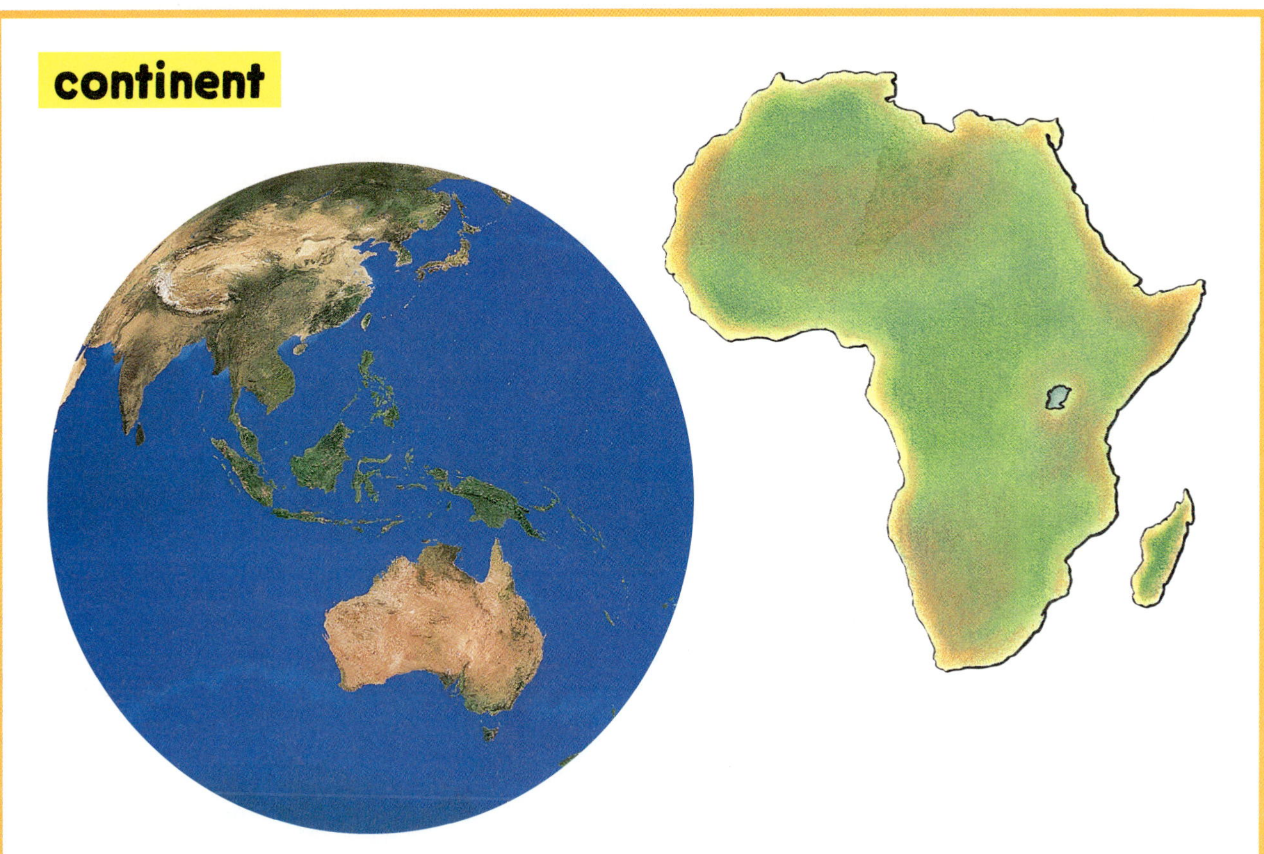

language

Se habla español.

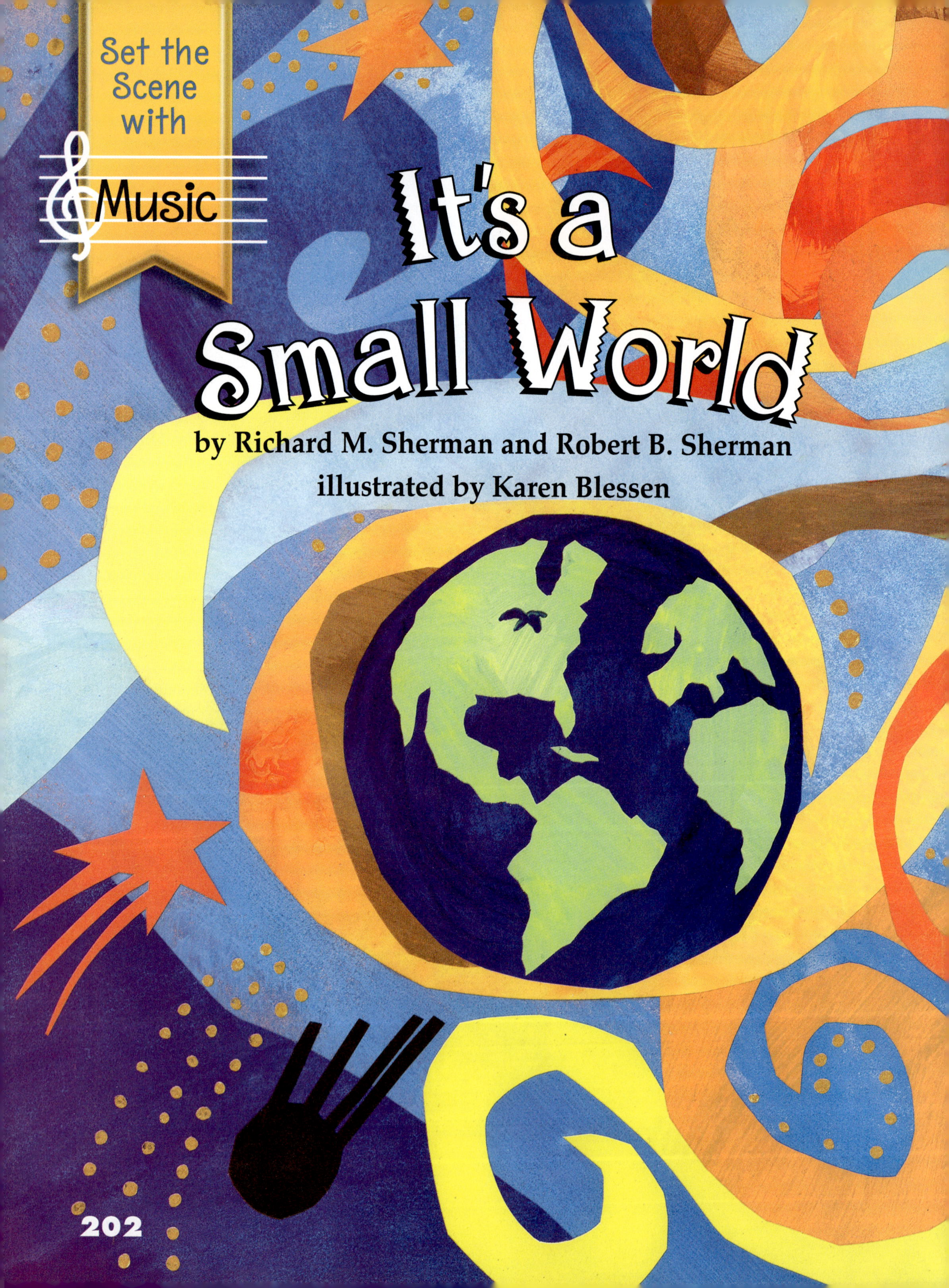

It's a Small World

by Richard M. Sherman and Robert B. Sherman

illustrated by Karen Blessen

It's a world of laughter,
a world of tears,
It's a world of hopes
and a world of fears.
There's so much that we share,
and it's time we're aware,
It's a small world after all.

It's a small world after all.
It's a small world after all.
It's a small world after all.
It's a small, small world.

There is just one moon
and one golden sun,
And a smile means friendship
to everyone.
Though the mountains divide
and the oceans are wide,
It's a small world after all.

LESSON 1

Where in the World Do People Live?

My grandma traveled around the world. The **world** is all the places and people on the Earth. Today we looked through Grandma's trunk in the attic. She showed me the things she brought back from the places she visited and the people she met.

Grandma showed me a dress she bought in Mexico. I found a fan from Korea. Grandma brought dolls from Russia.

Grandma took pictures of wild elephants in Tanzania. She visited some very old places in Greece.

Grandma made me feel as if I'd been around the world, too.

What Do You Know?

1. What is the world?
2. How can you learn about the world?

Use a Globe

Globe

You can find all the places in the world on a globe. A **globe** is a model of the Earth.

1 These drawings show the globe cut in half around the middle. They show the Northern Hemisphere and Southern Hemisphere. The word hemisphere means "half of the Earth."

Northern Hemisphere

2 A globe shows all the oceans and continents. A **continent** is a very large piece of land. North America is our continent. Find North America. Is it in the Northern Hemisphere or the Southern Hemisphere?

Southern Hemisphere

3 You can also cut a globe in half from top to bottom. The drawings below show the Western Hemisphere and Eastern Hemisphere. Find the place that is farthest north.

4 The place that is farthest north is the North Pole. The place that is farthest south is the South Pole. Is North America closer to the North Pole or the South Pole?

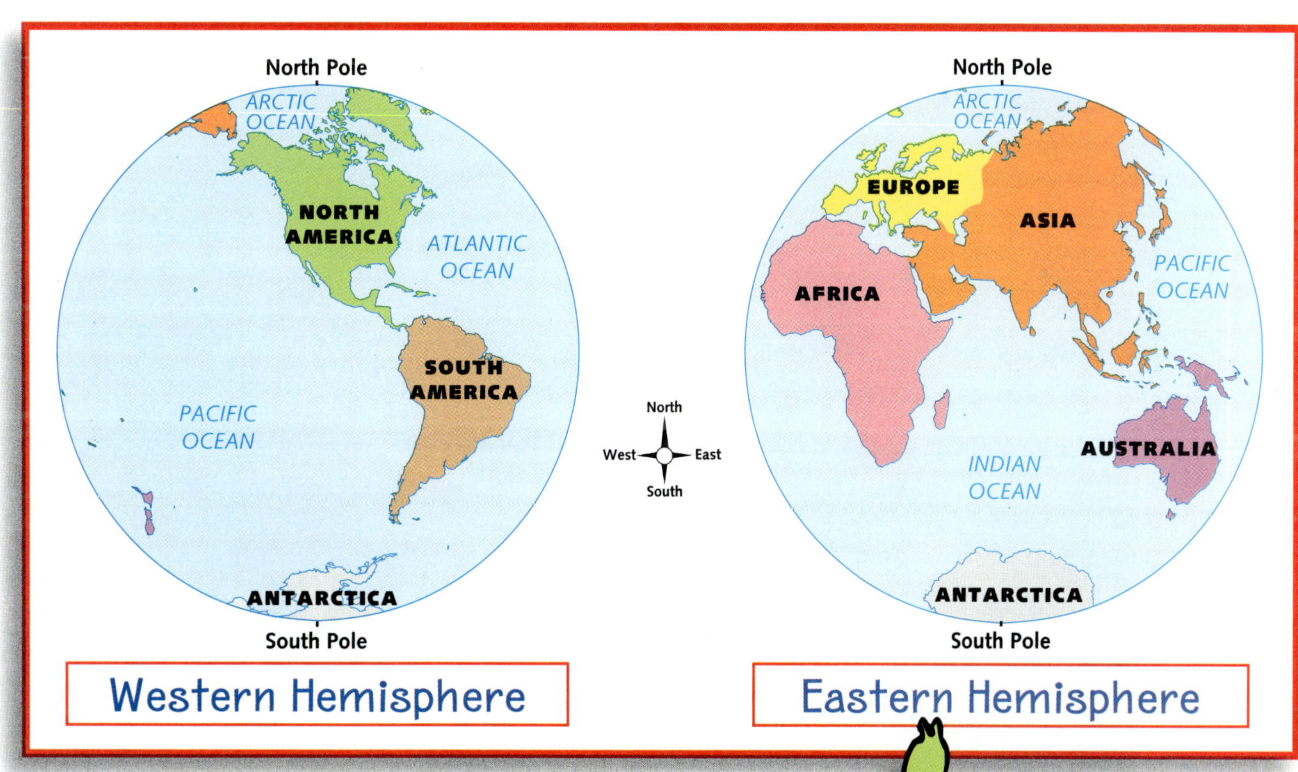

Think and Do

Name each continent. Then name each ocean.

LESSON 2

People Are People Everywhere

Our class is learning about children in other countries. People speak and write in many different languages. A **language** is the words we use. We have different ways of saying and doing things, but we are the same in many ways. Everyone has a way to say hello.

Jambo!
I live on a farm in Somalia.
As-salaam Alaykum!
I live in Jordan. My family has a pet goat.

¡Hola!
My grandmother is teaching me to weave in Peru.

Bonjour!
My friends and I enjoy going to a carnival in France.

Konnichiwa!
Families in Japan like to play in the park.

What Do You Know?

1. What is language?
2. How many ways can you say hello?

The Mouse in the Chest

by Aesop
illustrated by Dennis Hockerman

A mouse had lived all her life in a chest. She ate only the food she found there. The mouse was very happy in the chest. She never wanted to get out.

One day the lid was left open. The mouse came up to play. Then she fell out of the chest. She tried to get back in but could not.

The mouse ran all around the chest, looking for a way in. All she found was a bit of food. She popped it in her mouth. "I have never tasted such good food!" she cried. She looked around the room. "What a beautiful room!" cried the mouse.

The mouse looked out the window. "What a beautiful world!" she said. "How silly I have been! All this time I thought the only good things in life were in that chest!"

What Do YOU Know?

1. Why did the mouse say she had been silly?
2. What new things about the world have you learned?

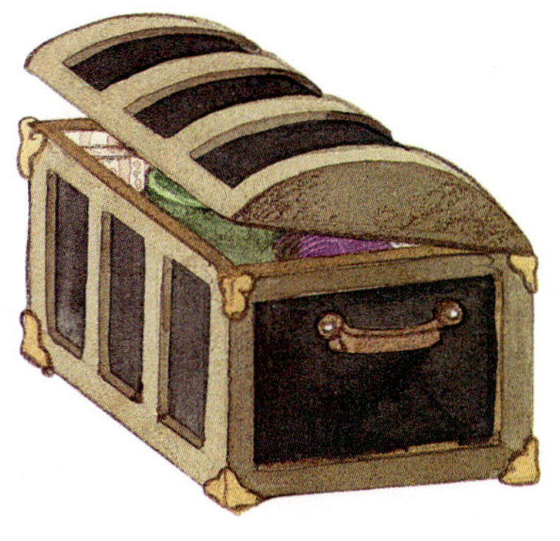

Tell What Might Happen

When the mouse came out of the chest, she saw many new things.

1. What new things does this boy see?
2. How do you think some of these things are used? What will the boy do with each one?
3. These things came from many countries. Why do you think people made them?

Think and Do

Draw a toy or game that has buttons to push. Ask classmates to guess what happens when someone pushes a button.

LESSON

4 People Everywhere Are Linked

People all over the world trade with one another. People in other countries buy goods that are made in the United States. And people in the United States buy goods that are made in other countries.

This picture is from a magazine in Japan. It shows an American camera that people in Japan buy.

Mexico sells many beautiful things to people in the United States. People in the United States buy silver, jewelry, and painted bowls from Mexico. Mexico also sells a lot of oil and food to the United States.

What Do You Know?

1. What things do people in the United States buy from Mexico?
2. Where do your things come from?

Chart and Graph Skills

Use a Bar Graph

Spencer has many toys and games. Some were made in different countries and were sent to the United States on ships or airplanes. Spencer wants to know how many came from each country. He makes a bar graph to show what he finds out. A **bar graph** helps you see how much or how many.

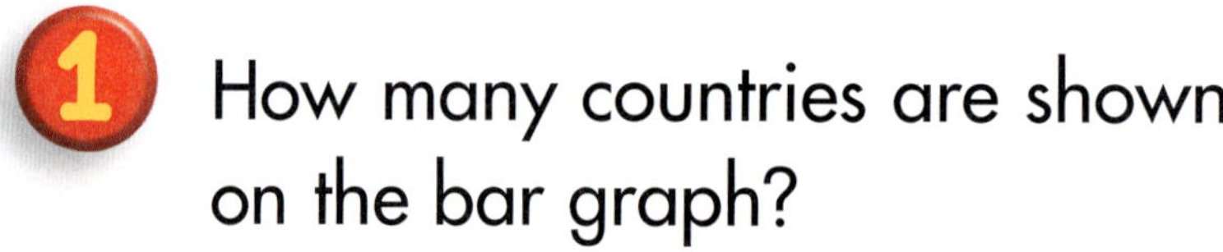

1 How many countries are shown on the bar graph?

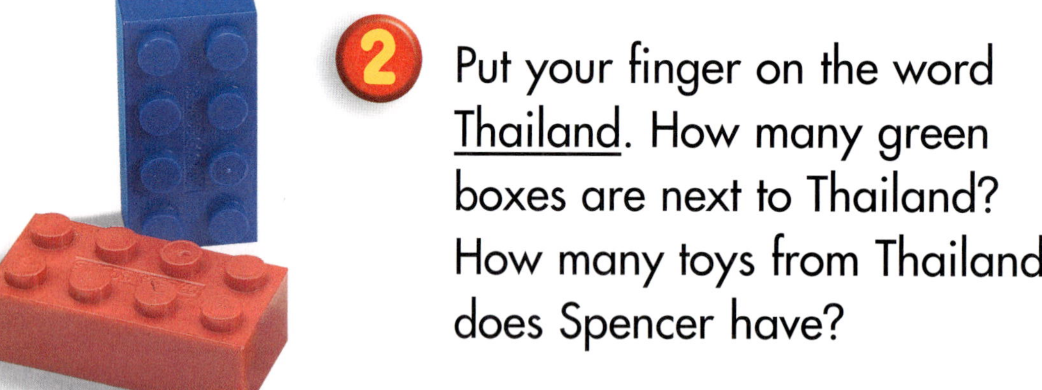

2 Put your finger on the word Thailand. How many green boxes are next to Thailand? How many toys from Thailand does Spencer have?

3 From which country does Spencer have five toys?

Think and Do

Which country did the most toys come from? Which country did the fewest come from?

LESSON

People Talk Around the World

Every day, people talk or write to share their feelings and ideas. This is called **communication**.

Long ago, people shared their ideas in different ways.

Clay Tablet

Today it is easier to share ideas. There are many ways to send messages. Children in schools around the world can even write to each other on computers.

Biography

Alexander Graham Bell invented the telephone. He also taught people who could not hear. Today many telephone companies are named after him.

World leaders work together to solve problems. Talking can help people learn more about one another. Communication helps people get along.

Mars Pathfinder

People look for better ways to communicate. Now we can talk to astronauts when they are in space. Machines in space can send pictures back to Earth. Scientists share what they learn with others around the world.

What Do You Know?

1. How does communication help people get along?
2. Name three ways you share ideas with others.

LESSON

We Share the Planet

People work together in many ways to solve problems on our planet. Our **planet** is the Earth. All kinds of animals share our planet with us. A zoo in California works with people around the world to help save animals in danger.

United States

San Francisco, California

My name is Emily. I talked with Dr. Eva Sargent at the San Francisco Zoo. Here are some things I found out.

Emily: Where is this cute animal from?

Dr. Sargent: This little animal is a lemur. It is from a country called Madagascar. We are working with zoos and in the forests there to save the lemurs. Other zoos around the world are helping, too.

Geography

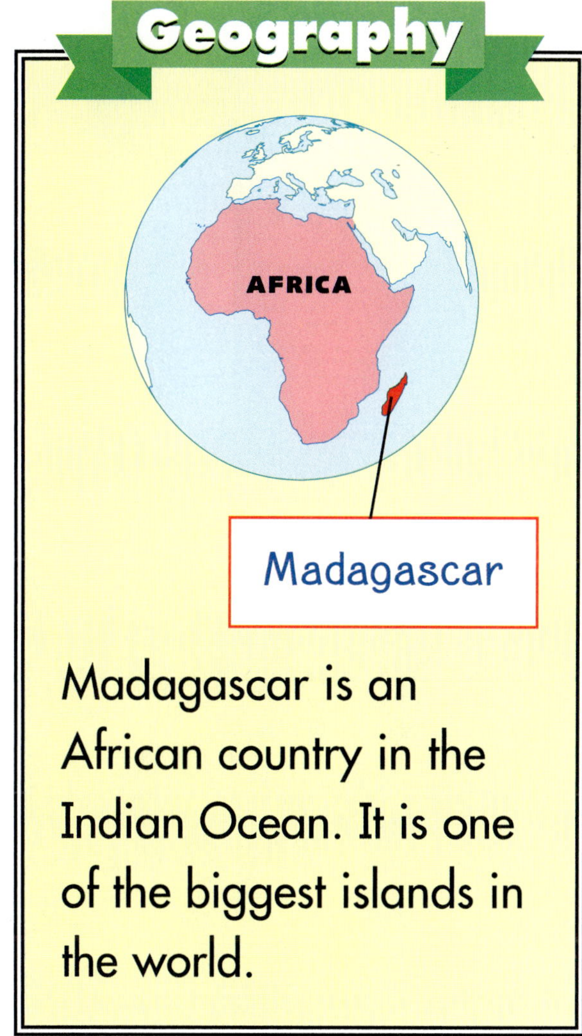

Madagascar is an African country in the Indian Ocean. It is one of the biggest islands in the world.

Emily: Why are the lemurs in danger?

Dr. Sargent: People in Madagascar need land for their crops and cattle. So they cut down the forests where the lemurs live.

Emily: How do you help animals at the zoo?

Dr. Sargent: We feed the animals and give them a place to live. We learn about them by reading books. We learn about them by watching what they do. People who visit our zoo learn about the animals and the places they came from.

Emily: Will these animals always live here?

Dr. Sargent: Some animals will always live here so that people can see them and learn to care about them. Others will stay here until their homes are safe. We have already sent some lemurs back to Madagascar.

What Do You Know?

1. How do the zoo workers help the animals?
2. Why should people around the world work together to solve problems?

Kids Meeting Kids

All children should have what they need. They should have food, clean water, and a safe home.

Kids Meeting Kids is a group that helps children get the things they need. Children and adults work to make life better for all children. They write letters to our country's leaders. They ask our leaders to make laws that protect children.

People who belong to Kids Meeting Kids also write to children in other countries. They are called pen pals for peace. Kids Meeting Kids wants to bring peace and fairness to all children.

What Can You Do?

- Join a pen pal club and learn about children in other countries.
- Write to your mayor. Find out how you can help children in your community.

Picture Summary

Look at the pictures. They will help you remember what you learned.

Talk About the Main Ideas

1. The world has many different and interesting people.
2. Children in other countries live, play, and work much as we do.
3. We trade goods with people around the world.
4. Communication helps people solve problems and get along.

Give a Speech Imagine that you are the President. You are meeting with leaders from other countries. What will you tell them about our country?

continent
globe
world
language

Use Vocabulary

Which word goes with each line?

1. a model of the Earth
2. all the places and people on the Earth
3. one of the largest pieces of land on the Earth
4. the words people use

Check Understanding

1. What country would you like to visit? Why?
2. On which continent is the country you want to visit? How would you get there?
3. How are children all over the world the same? How are they different?
4. What are some ways people communicate?

Think Critically

What is a problem that people all over the world are working to solve? Why is it a problem?

Apply Skills

How to Use a Bar Graph

Jamie got new clothes for school. Each square stands for one piece of clothing.

1. Which country did the most new clothes come from?
2. Which country did the fewest come from?
3. How many of Jamie's new clothes were made outside of the United States?

Do It Yourself

Draw a bar graph with three rows. Write three color names. Ask classmates which color they like best. Mark your graph to show which color each one chooses.

Apply Skills

Use a Globe

Find these things on the drawings of the globe. Write the name of each thing.

- the continent at the South Pole
- one ocean near North America
- two continents near Africa

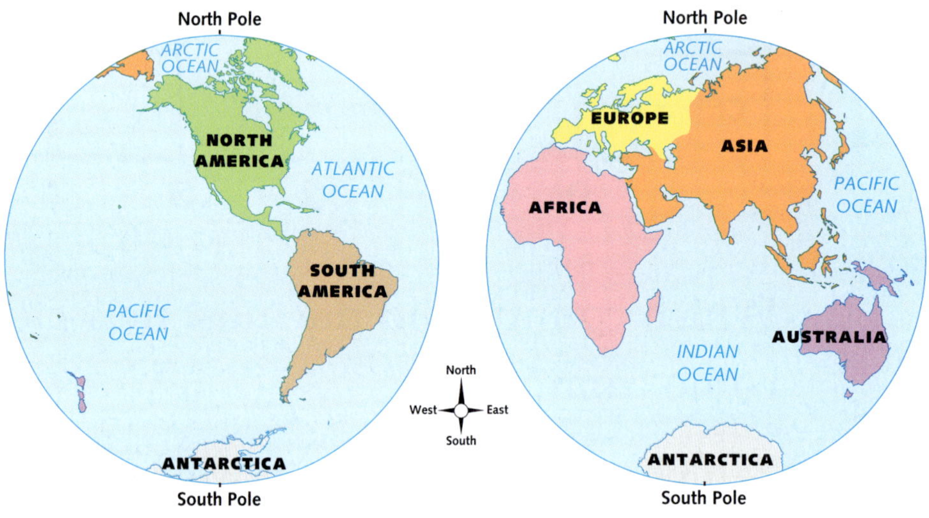

Tell What Might Happen

There are not very many rhinoceroses left in the world. Some people hunt them. Other people build houses too near where the rhinoceroses live. What might happen?

Unit Activity

Make an Our World Book

 Trace and cut out some paper circles.

 Make the book cover.

 Write things you have learned about the world. Add some pictures.

Visit the Internet at http://www.hbschool.com for additional resources.

Read More About It

All the Colors of the Earth by Sheila Hamanaka. Morrow. Meet children from many different places on the Earth.

At the Beach by Huy Voun Lee. Henry Holt. A mother teaches her son how to write some Chinese words in the sand.

Birthdays! Celebrating Life Around the World by Eve B. Feldman. Bridgewater. Find out how birthdays are celebrated around the world.

UNIT

7

Meeting People

Vocabulary

region
transportation
folktale
distance
inventor

Unit 7 Preview

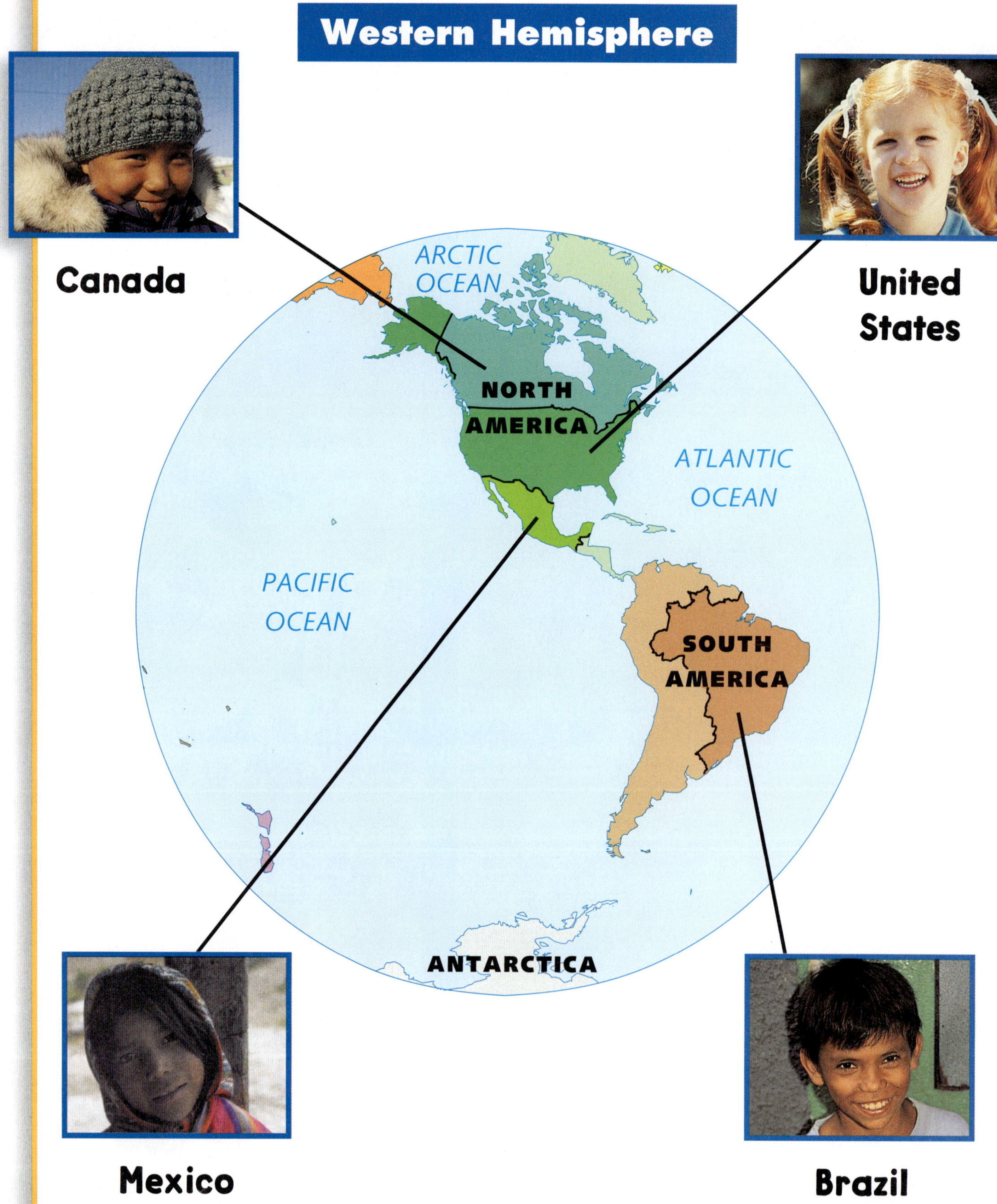

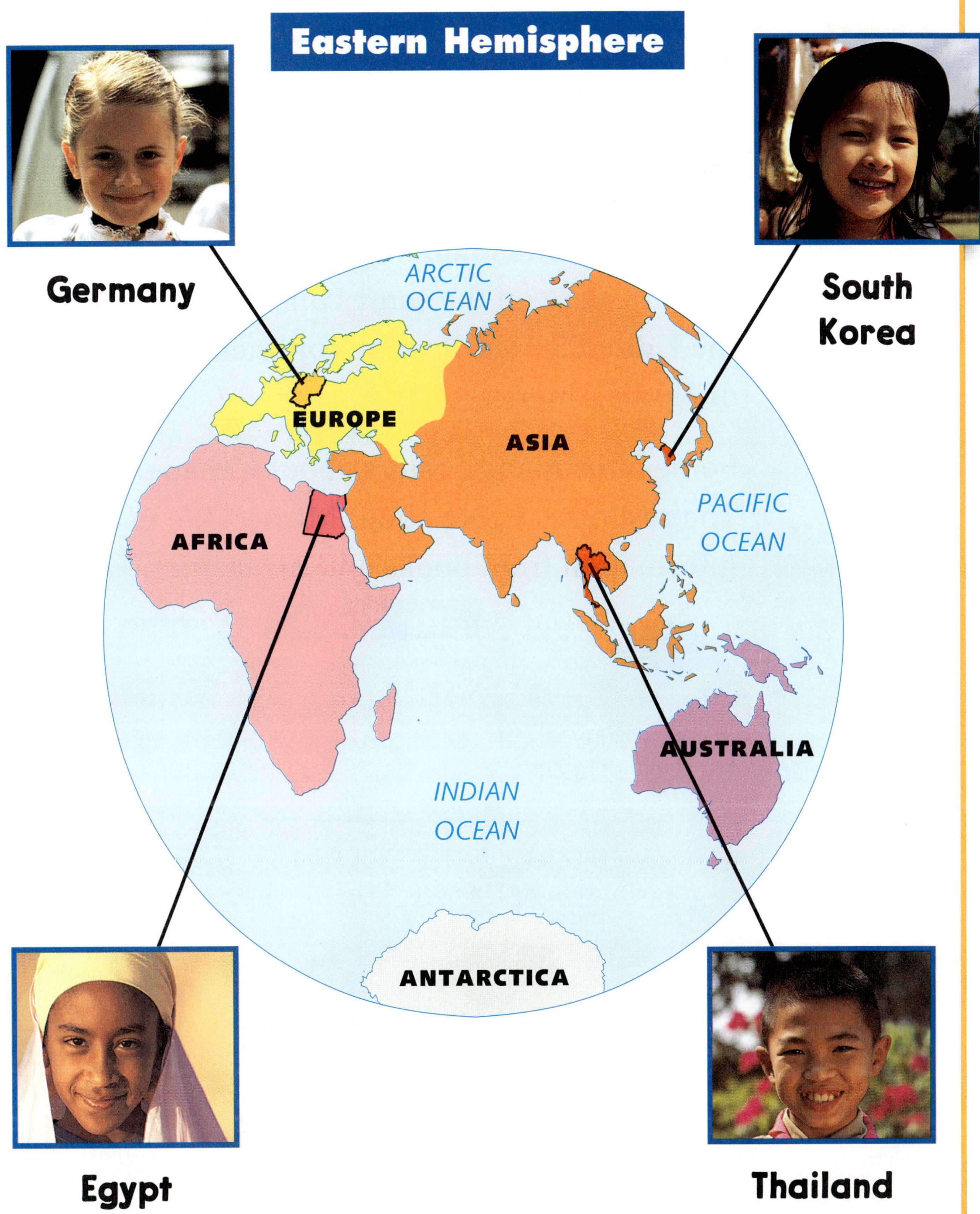
Eastern Hemisphere
Germany
South Korea
ARCTIC OCEAN
EUROPE
ASIA
AFRICA
PACIFIC OCEAN
AUSTRALIA
INDIAN OCEAN
ANTARCTICA
Egypt
Thailand

LESSON 1

Sharing a Continent

Our class is learning about Canada and Mexico. On the map, we see that these countries are on the same continent as the United States. It is the continent of North America.

Some of us made posters about Canada. The rest of us wrote about Mexico. We used information from books and magazines.

Canada's Land and People

Canada is like the United States. It has many different kinds of land. Lands near each other that are the same in some way make up a land **region**.

Canada's smallest land region is called the lowlands. This region has two important natural resources—farmland and water. A **natural resource** is an important resource found in nature. More people live in the lowlands than in any other part of Canada. The largest city, Toronto, is here.

Mexico's Land and People

Like the United States and Canada, Mexico has different land regions. The region in the north part is **desert**, or dry land. A desert does not have many plants because it does not rain much there.

Along the shores of Mexico there is good farmland. A **shore** is the land next to the water.

Geography

The saguaro cactus grows in the Sonoran Desert. This desert is in the south part of the United States and the north part of Mexico.

Mexico's largest land region is its high land. Crops grow well there. This land region has the most people and the largest city, Mexico City.

This large, high region has both flat land and mountains. South and east of Mexico City are two large volcanoes. West of Mexico City is the country's largest lake, Lake Chapala.

What Do You Know?

1. What kind of land is desert?
2. What is the land like where you live?

LESSON 2

People on Other Continents

People who live on other continents do some of the same things we do. They work, play, travel, and share their ideas. Let's take a trip through four countries. We will find out how people live today in each country.

Brazil

Brazil is a country in South America. In the cities, some people live in apartment buildings. Others live in small houses called favelas. In the country, people live in houses made from mud bricks.

In the cities, some people work in offices, shops, and factories. Others sell food or newspapers on the street. Outside the cities, some people grow fruits and vegetables to sell in markets. Others raise cattle and sheep on ranches.

Germany

Germany is a country in Europe. Many people there enjoy playing outdoors. The country's lakes and rivers are good for swimming and boating. In the winter, people ski on the snow-covered mountains. In the summer, they hike and camp in the same mountains.

People in Germany also like to play team sports. Soccer is a favorite for some.

Thailand

Thailand is a country in Asia. In Thailand people use many kinds of transportation. **Transportation** is any way of moving people or things from place to place. Some people get from place to place by walking, riding an animal, or riding a bicycle. Others travel by airplane, train, bus, car, and boat.

Egypt

Egypt is a country in Africa. People there have communicated for thousands of years by writing and drawing. Today they share their ideas by using a computer or telephone. They also write music and stories and make movies.

History

Long ago in Egypt, people used papyrus plants to make sails, cloth, and paper. To make paper, they cut the stems into thin strips. They pressed the strips together and dried them in the sun. Paper made from papyrus was used for many hundreds of years.

You have read about how people live on other continents. Some things they have always done will stay the same. They always will share ideas by talking and get from place to place by walking. Other things people do will change as they find new ways to communicate and to travel.

What Do You Know?

1. What is transportation?
2. How do you play and have fun?

Umbrellas and Straw Shoes

a Korean folktale
illustrated by Joung Un Kim

The stories people tell are important to them. One kind of story is the folktale. A **folktale** is a story from long ago that teaches a lesson. Folktales are passed down from great-grandparent to grandparent to parent to child.

Every country has its own folktales. They tell things the people of that country believe. Here is a folktale from Korea, a country in Asia.

Once there was a woman who had two sons. One son sold umbrellas. The other son sold straw shoes. When it did not rain, the woman worried about the son who sold umbrellas. People would not buy his umbrellas if it did not rain.

When the rain did fall, she worried about the son who sold straw shoes. People would not buy his straw shoes if the ground was muddy from rain.

The woman was always worried and never happy. Then a friend pointed out to her that whatever the weather, one son would always be selling his goods. The woman had to agree! After she learned to look on the bright side of things, she was happy all the time.

What Do You Know?

The main idea of a story tells what it is about. What is the main idea in this story?

LESSON

People in Different Times

We remember some people for the important things they have done. They are remembered because stories of their deeds are told and retold for many years.

Mrs. Kent's class chose seven famous people to learn about. The children formed fan clubs. Each club made trading cards to tell about its person.

Cleopatra was only eighteen when her father, the king of Egypt, died. She became the queen. She could speak several languages.

Cleopatra traveled all over Egypt to learn more about the people she ruled. She was the most powerful woman of her time.

Mansa Musa ruled a large part of Africa called Mali. Trade with other lands made Mali grow rich. People called Mansa Musa the King of Gold. He used his riches to build libraries, schools, and other buildings.

Augustus Caesar's real name was Octavian. Octavian was the leader of many lands. He made laws that were fair to everyone. He made the roads better and started mail delivery. He also ordered many bridges and beautiful buildings to be built.

Who Augustus Caesar
When more than 2,000 years ago
Where Rome, a city in Europe

Confucius was a teacher long ago in China. China was a very rich country, but its leaders were always fighting. Confucius believed people should get along. He taught ways to live in peace. Confucius said families and schools are very important. People still follow his teachings today.

Who Johannes Gutenberg
When 600 years ago
Where Germany, a country in Europe

Long ago, people wrote books by hand with pen and paper. That changed when Johannes Gutenberg built one of the first printing presses. A **printing press** stamps words onto paper. Thanks to Gutenburg, there were soon more books.

Marie Curie was a prize-winning scientist. She discovered a strong, shining metal. Doctors use this metal to help cure sickness. Because of the work Marie Curie did, other scientists have learned many new things.

Who Marie Curie
When 1867 to 1934
Where France, a country in Europe

Louis Pasteur was a scientist who helped people have healthier lives. He learned that some sickness is caused by germs. A **germ** is a living thing that is too small to be seen without a microscope. Louis Pasteur showed why hospitals should be kept clean and free of germs. He also showed how people could kill germs that get into milk and other foods.

Who Louis Pasteur
When 1822 to 1895
Where France, a country in Europe

What Do You Know?

1. Why do we know about famous people?
2. Why do you think it is important to wash hands?

LESSON 5

People Share Their History

Our class is going on a trip to a museum. A museum is a place where interesting objects from other times and places are kept for people to see. Today we will look at art from long ago. A guide will tell us about the art and the people who made it. We will learn how the people lived and what they believed.

The guide tells us that art often shows something about a group's religion. A **religion** is a belief in a God or gods and the way people show their belief. In this painting, the Mandan Indians are doing a hunting dance. They are asking their gods to help them find animals for food, clothing, and shelter.

Bull Dance Ma O-Kee Ceremony by George Catlin

Before people began to write and read, they told stories by carving or painting on rocks. They crushed plants and rocks of different colors to make their paints.

Cave paintings are found around the world. The painting in this cave in France shows animals running. Animals were used for food and clothing.

Biography

Jean-Marie Chauvet of France is a cave explorer. An explorer is a person who goes to a place that is little known. Jean-Marie Chauvet found a cave with more than 300 paintings on its walls. The cave was named for him.

Rock art is also found all over the world. A Navajo Indian in Utah carved these pictures long ago. Some people believe that the flute player is a god who helps plants grow.

Sculpture is another kind of art. A **sculpture** is a piece of art that is shaped from stone, clay, or other materials. Sculptures can be very large or very small. The Great Sphinx in Egypt is a very large sculpture. It shows an animal with the body of a lion and the head of a human. It may have been made to honor a king or a god.

Masks are another kind of sculpture. A mask is a covering that hides or protects the face. Most masks look like people or animals. Some of the oldest masks were made in Korea. Actors sometimes wear masks in plays.

The Hopi Indians of Arizona wear masks for special ceremonies. The masks often show the faces of their gods. The Indians may ask the gods to bring rain or to make the corn grow.

What Do You Know?

1. What can you find in a museum?
2. What can we learn from the art of people long ago?

Map and Globe Skills

Find Distance

You can use a map to help you find out how far apart places are.

1. Find the bar scale at the bottom of the map on page 269. The bar scale is like a ruler. You can use it to measure **distance**, or how far one place is from another. How many yards does one inch on the bar scale stand for? How many yards does two inches stand for?

2. Use a piece of paper to mark the distance between the • on the information desk and the • in the gift shop.

3. Then place the marked paper on the bar scale. How many yards are there between the marks? How many yards are there between the rooms?

Art Museum

Skills

Mask Room
Library
Painting Room
Sculpture Room
Elevators
Restaurant
Cave Art Room
Information Desk
Gift Shop

Bar Scale

0	1	2	3	4	5	6	7	8	9	10 yards
0	1	2	3	4	5	6	7	8	9 meters	

Think and Do

How far is it from the 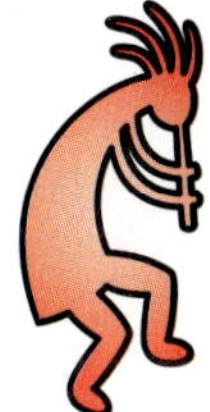 to the  ?

LESSON 6

Postcards from America

George Washington, the flag, the Statue of Liberty, and Independence Day are all important in our country's history. There are many other people, symbols, and holidays that are also important. Postcards here and on the following pages show some of the ways we remember each of them.

America's People

Betsy Ross may have helped sew a new flag for our country. That first flag had 13 stars and stripes because there were just 13 states then.

Sacagawea was a Shoshone Indian. She helped explorers Meriwether Lewis and William Clark communicate with the Shoshone Indians.

Harriet Tubman helped people who were slaves get to states where they could be free. She moved them from one hiding place to another on the long trip.

Jane Addams helped people who moved to Chicago from other countries. She started Hull House, where children could learn and play.

Lewis Latimer was an inventor who helped invent lightbulbs. An **inventor** is someone who thinks of or makes something for the first time.

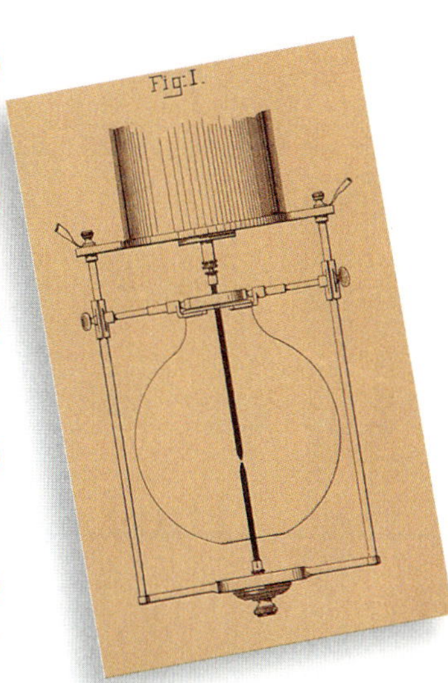

Orville and Wilbur Wright were inventors interested in transportation. They made and flew one of the first airplanes.

America's Symbols

The bald eagle is a powerful bird that is found only in North America. It is the national bird of the United States.

The Liberty Bell was first rung in July 1776 to celebrate the reading of the Declaration of Independence. The bell was rung for special events until it cracked.

The Lincoln Memorial is in Washington, D.C. Inside the memorial is a statue of President Abraham Lincoln.

The nation's Capitol building is in Washington, D.C. The leaders of our country meet there. The White House, also in Washington, D.C., is where the President works. He and his family live there, too.

Florida's capitol building is in Tallahassee. Florida's leaders meet there.

America's Holidays

On Martin Luther King, Jr., Day, we honor the man who worked for the rights of all Americans.

January

February

On Presidents' Day we celebrate what all Presidents have done for our country.

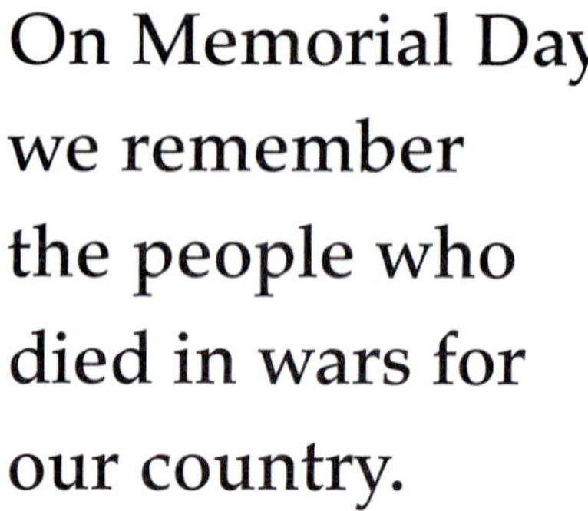

May

On Memorial Day we remember the people who died in wars for our country.

On Flag Day people fly the American flag and remember why it is important.

June

September

On Labor Day we honor the working people of the United States.

On Veterans Day we honor all the people who have fought in wars to protect our country.

November

What Do You Know?

1. What are some of the ways we honor people?
2. What kinds of statues, memorials, or monuments does your community have?

Solving Problems

Taking Care of Our Treasures

Americans are proud of their parks, statues, and places where important things happened long ago. Ellis Island is one of these important places. It tells something about our country's history.

Long ago, people from all over the world sailed to our country and landed at Ellis Island. They came to the United States to have a better life. Today many people visit the museum on Ellis Island.

What Would You Do?

Think about Ellis Island and about places of interest where you live.

- How can you help save these places for others to visit?
- What are some rules good citizens follow when they visit important places?
- What would you do if you saw a classmate breaking a rule on a field trip to such a place?

Brainstorm

Use Vocabulary

Which word goes with each box?

folktale	**inventor**
region	**transportation**

1. lands near each other that are the same in some way
2. someone who thinks of or makes something for the first time
3. ways of moving people or things from place to place
4. a story from long ago that teaches a lesson

Check Understanding

1. Name two natural resources found in Canada. Why are they important?
2. What can you learn about people from their art?
3. Who do we honor on Veterans Day?

Think Critically

How do inventors change people's lives?

Apply Skills

Identify Hemispheres

Western Hemisphere

Eastern Hemisphere

Northern Hemisphere

Southern Hemisphere

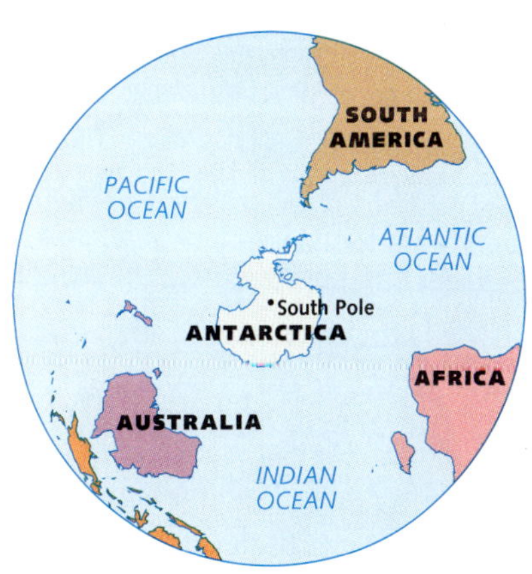

1. In which two hemispheres is Asia?
2. In which two hemispheres is North America?

Apply Skills

Find Distance

1. How far is it from the giraffe to the bear?

2. How far is it from the alligator to the bird?

Sunshine State Zoo

Tigers
Birds
Giraffes
Bears
Alligators
Zoo Hospital
Front Gate

Bar Scale
0 10 20 30 40 50 yards
0 10 20 30 40 meters

Unit Activity

Make a Family Crest

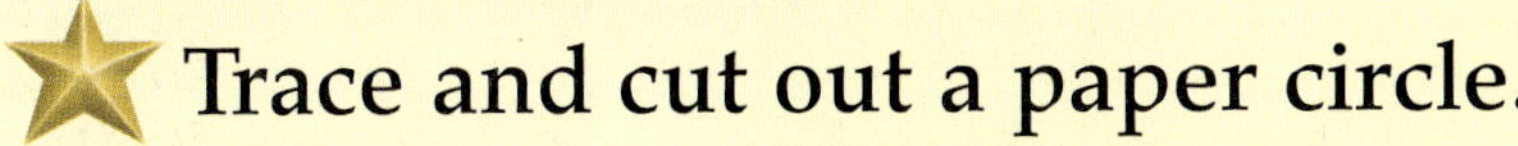

- Trace and cut out a paper circle.
- Think of three things that are important in your family's history. Draw these things on the circle.

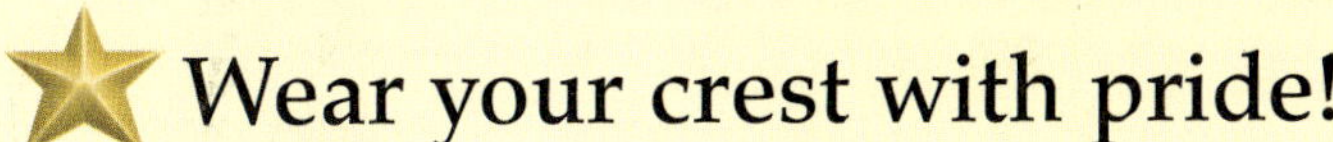

- Wear your crest with pride!

Visit the Internet at http://www.hbschool.com for additional resources.

Read More About It

All Kinds of Children by Norma Simon. Albert Whitman. This book shows how children around the world are both the same and different.

All the Way to Morning by Marc Harshman. Cavendish. A boy thinks about what children around the world hear before they go to sleep.

Different Just Like Me by Lori Mitchell. Charlesbridge. A girl sees how people are different from her but also the same in many ways.

Glossary

address
A way to find a home or building. (page 48)

apartment
One kind of home. (page 47)

bar graph
A picture that shows how many or how much. (page 220)

calendar
A chart that shows the days, weeks, and months of the year. (page 170)

celebrate
What people do to make an important day special. (page 69)

change
Something that happens to make things different. (page 50)

choice

What people pick instead of something else. (page 63)

communication

Sharing ideas with others. (page 222)

citizen

A member of a community. (page 176)

community

A place where people live and the people who live there. (page 86)

city

A large community where people live, work, and play. (page 86)

continent

One of the largest bodies of land on the Earth. (page 206)

country

A land and the people who live in that land. (page 162)

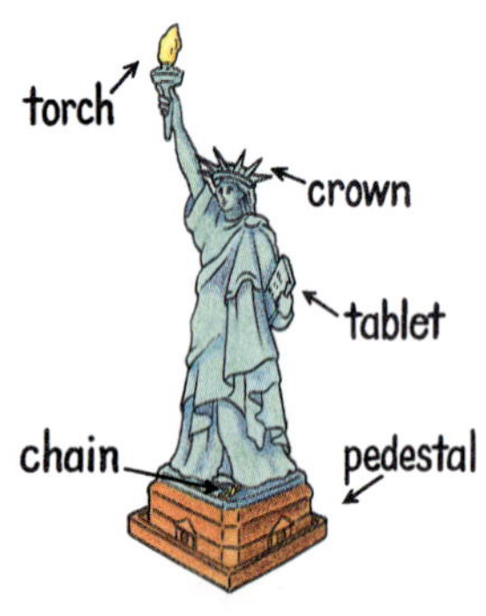

diagram

A drawing that shows the parts of something. (page 188)

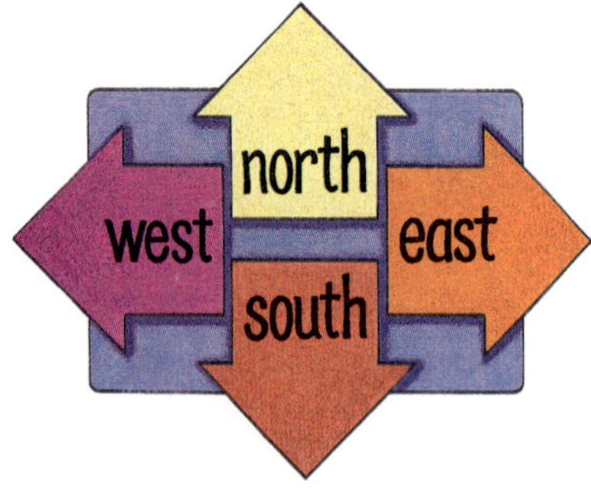

direction

North, south, east, or west. (page 94)

factory

A place where things are made. (page 138)

family

A group of people who care for one another. (page 46)

farm

A place where people raise food and other resources. (page 130)

flag

A symbol that stands for a country. (page 161)

globe

A model of the Earth. (page 206)

forest

A place where many trees grow. (page 128)

goods

Things that people make or grow. (page 102)

friends

People that you like and know very well. (page 15)

group

A number of people doing an activity together. (page 26)

hero

A person who is known for doing something special. (page 175)

hill

High land that is not as high as a mountain. (page 125)

history

The story of what has happened in a place. (page 172)

holiday

A time to celebrate. (page 69)

job

The work a person does. (page 18)

lake

A body of water that has land around it. (page 125)

language

The words people use. (page 208)

learn

To find out something new. (page 12)

law

A rule that everyone must follow. (page 178)

map

A drawing that shows where places are. (page 16)

leader

A person who helps a group plan what to do. (page 92)

map key

A list of the symbols that are used on a map. (page 20)

money

Coins or bills that people trade for things they want. (page 62)

mountain

The highest kind of land. (page 125)

needs

Things people cannot live without. (page 46)

neighborhood

A small part of a community. (page 86)

ocean

A very large body of salty water. (page 125)

pictograph

A picture that uses symbols to show numbers of things. (page 142)

plain

Land that is mostly flat. (page 125)

President

The leader of the United States. (page 175)

planet

A body in space, like the Earth, that moves around the sun. (page 226)

recycle

To make something old into something new. (page 145)

post office

A building where workers sort the mail. (page 90)

resource

Something people use that comes from the Earth. (page 128)

river

A long body of water that flows through the land. (page 125)

season

One of the four parts of the year—winter, spring, summer, and fall. (page 170)

rule

What you must or must not do. (page 30)

services

Things people do to help others. (page 92)

school

A place for learning. (page 14)

shelter

A place to live. (page 46)

state
A part of a country. (page 163)

house

symbol
A picture that stands for something real. (page 20)

How Much We Weigh

Name	Weight
Fred	48 lb
Juan	53 lb
Pete	61 lb

table
A list of things in groups. (page 104)

teacher
A person who helps people learn. (page 15)

First shoes
First tricycle
First day of school
1 year
2 years
3 years
4 years
5 years

time line
A line that shows when things happened. (page 60)

vote
A choice that gets counted. (page 176)

wants
Things people would like to have. (page 62)

world
A name for the Earth and everything on it. (page 204)

Credits

Photo Credits:
Key: (t) top; (b) bottom; (l) left; (r) right; (c) center; (fg) foreground; (bg) background

Table of Contents,
iii, Tony Stone Images; iv, Richard Hutchings; v, Liaison Agency; vi, Ed Malitsky/Liaison Agency; vii (both), Art Resource, NY; viii, Superstock

Unit 1:
6-7, Tom Stewart/The Stock Market; 6 (bl), Frozen Images; 8 (tr), David R. Frazier/Photo Researchers; 8 (tl), John W. Warden/Superstock; 8 (bl), Harcourt; 9 (tl), Superstock; 9 (tr), Chuck Savage/The Stock Market; 9 (bl), Frozen Images; 12-13, Rich Franco/Harcourt; 13 (tl), Stephanie Fitzgerald/Peter Arnold, Inc.; 13 (tr), David Young-Wolff/PhotoEdit; 13 (br) Michael Groen Photography; 14, 16-18, Rich Franco/Harcourt; 15 (tr), Michael Groen Photography; 19 (br), Tony Freeman/ PhotoEdit; 18-19, Tony Stone Images; 19 (bl), Richard Hutchings; 19 (tr), Michael Groen Photography; 22-23, Lillian Gee/Picture It; 23 (tr), The Country School by Winslow Homer/ 1871 /The Saint Louis Art Museum; 23 (cr), Brown Brothers; 24 (bl), Michael Groen Photography; 24, (tr) Jonathan Klein/Klein Postcard; 25 (cr), Michael Groen Photography; 25 (cl), Corbis; 26, Rich Franco/Harcourt; 26, Harcourt; 27 (both), Rich Franco/Harcourt; 27, Harcourt; 28-29, Lillian Gee/ Picture It; 30-31, Rich Franco/Harcourt; 31 (tr), Chip Henderson/Tony Stone Images; 31 (tl), Tony Stone Images; 31 (br), PhotoEdit; 32-33, Chuck Kneyse/Black Star/Harcourt; 33, Michael Groen Photography; 38, Michael Groen Photography; 39 (tr), Michael Groen Photography

Unit 2:
40-41, Lillian Gee/Picture It; 40 (bl), Richard Hutchings; 42 (tl), Richard Hutchings; 42 (tr), Maria Paraskevas/ Harcourt; 42 (bl), Victoria Bowen/Harcourt; 42 (br), Michael Groen Photography; 42 (t), Harcourt; 43 (cl), J. Graham/H. Armstrong Roberts; 43 (br), Guy Marche/ FPG; 46 (t), Picture It; 46 (c), Michael Groen Photography; 46 (cl), Ron Anstring/Photo Researchers; 47 (cr), Michael Groen Photography; 47 (tl), Myrleen Ferguson/PhotoEdit; 47-48, Rich Franco/Harcourt; 60-61 (all), Fran Antmann; 62-63, Rich Franco/Harcourt; 63 (tl), Harcourt; 63 (tr), 64, Rich Franco/Harcourt; 65 (l), Steve Wisbauer/Still Life Stock; 65 (tr), Superstock; 65 (br), FPG; 66 (both), Plymouth Plantation; 67 (br), Aaron Haupt/Photo Researchers; 67-68, Plymouth Plantation; 69 (c), Blair Seitz/Photo Researchers; 69 (t), Plymouth Plantation; 69 (b), Superstock; 70-71, Plymouth Plantation; 72-73, Courtesy of Tammy Bubb; 79, Michael Groen Photography

Unit 3:
80-81, Lillian Gee/Picture It; 80 (bl), Superstock; 82 (tl), Rafael Macia/Photo Researchers; 82 (tc), Superstock; 82 (tr), Michael Groen Photography; 82 (bl), Fran Antmann; 82 (cl), Superstock; 82 (cr), Harcourt; 82 (br), Terry D. Sinclair/Harcourt; 83 (tl), Colin Hackley/Tampa Tribune/Silver Image; 83 (cr & cl), Harcourt; 83 (tr), Bob Daemmrich/Stock, Boston; 83 (cr & br), Michael Groen Photography; 83, Michael Groen Photography; 86-87, Superstock; 86 (l), Rich Franco/Harcourt; 87 (r), Richard Brunoff/The Stock Market; 87 (tl), Rich Franco/ Harcourt; 88 (tl), John Terrence Turner/FPG; 88 (b), Toyohiro Yamada/FPG; 89 (tr), PhotoEdit; 89 (bl), Liaison Agency; 88-89 (t), Michael Groen Photography; 90 (cl), Eric Roth/The Picture Cube; 90 (cr), Bob Daemmrich/The Image Works; 90 (b), Courtesy of Korean Airlines; 91 (bl & br), Courtesy of Korean Airlines; 91 (t), Courtesy of the U.S. Postal Service; 92 (tr), Harcourt; 92 (bl), Courtesy of the Orange County Registrar; 92 (br), 93 (t), Keith Skelton/Black Star/ Harcourt; 93 (b), Courtesy of City of Santa Ana Parks; 96, Lillian Gee/Picture It; 97, Michael Groen Photography; 97 (tl, tr & bl), Courtesy of Joan Murphy/ Clayton State College; 97 (br), Rob Nelson/Black Star/ Harcourt; 98 (tl), Courtesy of John Wieland Homes; 98 (bl), Dennis McDonald/PhotoEdit; 98 (tr & br), Courtesy of Bruno's Supercenter; 99 (l), Rob Nelson/Black Star/Harcourt; 99 (r), Corbis; 100, Lillian Gee/Picture It; 100-101 (t), Alex MacLean/Landslides; 101 (b), David R. Frazier/Photo Researchers; 102 (tl & bl), Michael Groen Photography; 102 (br) & 103, Rich Franco/ Harcourt; 104, Michael Groen Photography; 105 (all), Terry Sinclair/Harcourt; 106 (tr), Michael Groen Photography; 106 (tl), Photri; 106 (b), Steven Gottleib/ FPG; 107 (b), Photodisc; 107 (tl), Chromosohm/Stock, Boston; 107 (tr), Rich Franco/Harcourt; 108 (bl), Porterfield/Chickering/Photo Researchers; 108 (br), Rich Franco/Harcourt; 108 (tl), Photri; 109 (cl), Culver Pictures; 109 (tr), NASA; 109 (b), Frank Siteman/Stock, Boston; 09 (tl), Rich Franco/Harcourt; 110-111, Courtesy of Hillside Elementary School

Unit 4:
118-119, Jerry Howard/Stock, Boston; 118 (bl), Superstock; 120 (tl), Frozen Images; 120 (bl), Fridmar Damm/Leo de Wys; 120 (tr), Tom Stewart/The Stock Market; 120 (br), Don Mason/The Stock Market; 121 (tl), Roger du Buisson/The Stock Market; 121 (bl), Michael Groen Photography; 121 (tr), David R. Frazier/ Frozen Images; 121 (br), Lawrence Migdale; 125 (#1), Luis Padilla/The Image Bank; 125 (#2), William Johnston/Stock, Boston; 125 (#3), Alan Kearney/FPG; 125 (#4), Richard Johnston/FPG; 125 (#5), Gary Irving/ Tony Stone Images; 125 (#6), Robert Daemmrich/Tony Stone Images; 128 (l), Richard Dunoff/The Stock Market; 128 (r), Glen Allison/Tony Stone Images; 129 (t), Corbis; 129 (b), Lois Bernstein/Liaison Agency; 130 (l), Stephen R. Swinburne/Stock, Boston; 130 (c), Visual Horizons/FPG; 130 (t), Fridmar Damm/Leo de Wys; 131 (tr), Miami Herald; 131 (tl), Michael P. Godomski/Photo Researchers; 131 (br), D. Young-Wolfe/ PhotoEdit; 132, Richard Hutchings; 133 (t), Michael Collier; 133 (bl), Water Resources Center Archives/UC Berkeley, CA; 133 (br), Brown Bros.; 134 (tr), Tom Campbell/FPG; 134 (c), Andrew Pernick/USBR; 134 (tl), Michael Groen Photography; 134 (b), Brian Smith/ Liaison Agency; 134-135 (tl), Michael Collier; 135 (tr), Russ Bishop Photography; 135, (br), Michael Groen Photography; 136-137 (t), Tom Walker/Stock, Boston; 136-137 (bl), Michael Goldman/FPG; 137 (br), Kim Hart/Black Star; 139 (t), John Warden/Tony Stone Images; 139 (b), Ed Malitsky/Liaison Agency; 140 (all), Christian Vioujard/Liaison Agency; 141 (t), Courtesy of Cabot Cheese; 141 (b), Joseph Nettis/Stock, Boston; 142, Michael Groen Photography; 145 (tl), Annette Stahl/Harcourt; 145 (tr), Rich Franco/Harcourt; 145 (br), Tim Davis/Photo Researchers; 146, Michael Groen

Photography; 148-149, Lawrence Migdale; 149 (bl), Michael Groen Photography; 154 (t), Ron Sanford/ International Stock; 154 (b), Michael Groen Photography; 155, Harcourt

Unit 5:

156-157, Allen Russell/Index Stock; 156 (bl), National Portrait Gallery/Smithsonian/Art Resource; 158 (tl), Harcourt; 158 (tr), Superstock; 159 (tl), National Portrait Gallery/Smithsonian/Art Resource, NY; 159 (tr), John Trumbull/Wadsworth Atheneum, Hartford; 159 (cr), Peter Gridley/FPG; 159 (bl), Art Attack/Photo Researchers; 159 (br), Michal Heron/The Stock Market; 162-163, Harcourt; 166 (l), Rob Crandall/Stock, Boston; 167 (tr), The Granger Collection; 168 (r), Michael P. Gadomski/Photo Researchers; 168 (c), Marcel Ehrhard/ Liaison Agency; 168 (l), Bonnie Sue/Photo Researchers; 169 (r), Telegraph Color Library/FPG; 169 (l), Rob Crandall/FPG; 169 (c), Magnus Rew/Tony Stone Images; 171 (t), Rother/Unicef; 171 (bl), Corbis; 171 (br), National Portrait Gallery/Smithsonian/Art Resource, NY; 172 (l), John Trumbull/Wadsworth Atheneum, Hartford; 172-173, Rich Franco/Harcourt; 174 (tl), Eastman Johnson/Art Resource, NY; 174-175, Rich Franco/ Harcourt; 175 (c), Rich Franco/Harcourt; 175 (tr), National Portrait Gallery/Smithsonian/Art Resource, NY; 175 (tl), Gilbert Stuart/Superstock; 177, Lillian Gee/ Picture It; 178, Victoria Bowen/Harcourt; 188, L. Fisher/ Postcard Factory; 190 (t), Sheri O'Neal/Harcourt; 190 (b), Santo Fabio/Black Star/Harcourt; 191, Santo Fabio/ Black Star/Harcourt; 191, Sal Di Marco/Black Star; 192 (bl), Tom Tracy/FPG; 192 (tl), Jacob Taposchaner/FPG; 193 (tr), D.C. Lowe/FPG; 193 (cr), Peter Gridley/FPG; 193 (br), Rob Crandall/FPG; 197, Harcourt

Unit 6:

198-199, Lillian Gee/Picture It; 198 (c), Victoria Bowen/ Harcourt; 198 (bl) & 200 (tr), NASA; 200 (b), Victoria Bowen/Harcourt; 201 (tl), World Sat Int'l/Science Source/Photo Researchers; 201 (cl), Donald Dietz/ Stock, Boston; 201 (br), Fran Antmann; 201 (bl), Michael Groen Photography/; 204, Victoria Bowen/ Harcourt; 204-205, Superstock; 205 (tr), Tony Stone Images; 205 (cl) & (bl), PhotoEdit; 206, Victoria Bowen/ Harcourt; 208, Charlene Daley/Valen Photos; 209 (t), Betty Press/Woodfin Camp & Associates; 209 (b), George Chan/Tony Stone Images; 210 (t), Superstock; 210 (b), FPG; 211 (t), Tony Stone Images; 211 (b), Michael Groen Photography; 216-217, Lillian Gee/ Picture It; 218 (l), Kodak; 218-219, Michael Groen Photography; 219 (r), Trade Commission of Mexico; 220, Terry Sinclair/Harcourt; 222 (b), Lillian Gee/Picture It; 222 (tl), Michael Groen Photography; 222 (tr), Erich Lessing/Art Resource, NY; 223 (t, bl & br), Lillian Gee/ Picture It; 223 (tr), Corbis; 224-225 (b), Lillian Gee/ Picture It; 224 (b), Richard Berenholtz/The Stock Market; 224 (c), SPL/Photo Researchers; 22 (t), Ron Haviv/SABA; 225 (t), Ted Soqui/Sygma; 225 (cr), Steve Wisbauer/Still Life Stock; 226 (bl), Rich Franco/Harcourt; 226 (br),Robert Foothorap/Black Star/Harcourt; 227 (tl), Dean Lee/Wildlife Collection; 227 (bl), Courtesy of Dennis Meredith/Duke University; 228 (all),Robert Foothorap/Black Star/Harcourt; 229, Martin Harvey/ Wildlife Collection; 230-231, Courtesy of Mary Sochet; 231 (br), Victoria Bowen/Harcourt; 236 (bl), Joe McDonald/Animals Animals

Unit 7:

238, Wolfgang Kaehler Photography; 238-239 (bg), Ron Karten/Omni-Photo Communications; 238-239 (fg), Harcourt; 240 (tl), Wolfgang Kaehler Photography; 240 (tr), Tom McCarthy/The Picture Cube; 240 (bl), Buddy Mays/Corbis; 240 (br), David R. Frazier; 241 (tl), Travelpix/FPG; 241 (tr), Wolfgang Kaehler Photography; 241 (bl), Richard Nowitz; 241 (br), Josef Beck/FPG; 242-243, Harcourt; 243 (tl & bl), Wolfgang Kaehler Photography; 243 (r), Corbis; 244 (tl), J.P. Courau/D. Donne Bryant; 244 (tr), F. Gohier/Photo Researchers; 244 (b), Corbis; 245 (tl), Peter Chartrand/D. Donne Bryant; 245 (tr & b) Robert Frerck/Woodfin Camp & Associates; 246, Harcourt; 247 (t), David R. Frazier; 247 (b), Luiz C. Marigo/Peter Arnold, Inc.; 248 (t), Adam Woolfitt/Corbis; 248 (bl), Mitchell Layton/Newsport Photography; 248 (br), Harcourt; 249 (t & br), David R. Frazier; 249 (bl) Will & Deni McIntyre/Photo Researchers; 250 (t), Richard T. Nowitz; 250 (bl), Harcourt; 250 (br), Gregory G. Dimijian/Photo Researchers; 251 & 256, Harcourt; 257 (b), Harcourt; 258 (t), Bibliotheque Nationale, Paris; 258 (b), Art Resouece, NY; 259 (t), The Granger Collection, New York; 259 (b), Harcourt; 260 (t), The Granger Collection, New York; 260 (b), Corbis; 261, Brian Wilson/Ancient Art and Architecture Collection; 262, Harcourt; 263 (t), Christie's Images; 263 (b), National Museum of American Art, Washington D.C./Art Resource, NY; 264 (t), Douglas Mazonwicz/ Bruce Coleman, Inc.; 264 (b), Jerome Wyckoff/Earth Scenes; 265 (t), Jean-Marie Chauvet/Sygma; 265 (c), Tom Bean; 265 (b), Marilyn "Angel" Wynn/Sun Valley Video & Photography; 266 (t), Wolfgang Keahler Photography; 266 (b), Erich Lessing/Art Resource, NY; 267 (t), Martha Cooper/Peter Arnold, Inc.; 267 (c), Marilyn "Angel" Wynn/Sun Valley Video & Photography; 267 (b), Ray Manley/Superstock; 270, Harcourt; 271 (bg), Harcourt; 271 (t), Francis G. Mayer/Corbis; 271 (bl), John Reddy/Courtesy of the Montana Historical Society; 271 (br), The United States Mint; 272 (t & b), Corbis; 273 (tl), The Queens Borough Public Library; 273 (tr), Harcourt; 273 (bl), American Stock/Archive Photos; 273 (br), Corbis; John Warden/Tony Stone Images; 274 (cl), Ed Wheeler/The Stock Market; 274 (cr), Lester Lefkowitz/The Stock Market; 274 (b), Lance Nelson/The Stock Market; 275 (t), Mark E. Gibson/ Dembinsky Photo Associates; 275 (c), John Skowronski Photography; 275 (b), David G. Houser/Corbis; 276, Archive Photos; 276, The Corcoran Gallery of Art/ Corbis; 276, William Johnson/Stock, Boston; 276, AP/ Wide World Photos; 277 (t), Bill Bachmann/PhotoEdit; 277 (b), Viviane Moos/The Stock Market; 279 (t), Corbis; 279 (br) Paraskevas Photography

All maps by MapQuest.com, Inc. (formerly known as GeoSystems) except:

20-21, 37, 49, 94-95, 115, 126-127, 170, 268, 282, Rita Lascaro

Illustration Credits:

Unit 1

10-11, Stacey Schuett; 34-35, Lynne Cravath

Unit 2

44-45, Holly Cooper; 50-59, David Soman; 74-75, Cathy Diefendorf

Unit 3
84-85, Doug Bowles; 112-113, Larry McEntire

Unit 4
122-123, Elisa Kleven; 138-141, Liz Allen; 150-151, Stacey Schuett

Unit 5
160-161, Barbara Maslen; 166-167, Pat DeWitt Grush; 180-187, Neil Waldman; 192-193, Hugo Cruz Moro

Unit 6
202-203, Karen Blessen; 212-215, Dennis Hockerman; 232-233, Viv Eisner-Hess

Unit 7
252-255, Joung Un Kim

For permission to reprint copyrighted material, grateful acknowledgment is made to the following sources:

Atheneum Books for Young Readers, Simon & Schuster Children's Publishing Division: America the Beautiful by Katharine Lee Bates, illustrated by Neil Waldman. Illustrations copyright © 1993 by Neil Waldman.

Barron's Educational Series, Inc.: Cover illustration from *The Four Elements: Water* by Carme Solé Vendrell and J. M. Parramón. © by Parramón Ediciones, S. A. First English language edition published in 1985 by Barron's Educational Series, Inc.

BridgeWater Books, an imprint of Troll Communications L.L.C.: Cover illustration by Paintbrush Diplomacy from *Birthdays: Celebrating Life Around the World* by Eve B. Feldman. Text copyright © 1996 by Eve B. Feldman; illustration copyright © 1996 by Paintbrush Diplomacy.

Carolrhoda Books, Inc., Minneapolis, MN: Cover illustration by Peter E. Hanson from *Buttons for General Washington* by Peter and Connie Roop. Copyright © 1986 by Carolrhoda Books, Inc.

Marshall Cavendish: Cover illustration by Felipe Dávalos from *All the Way to Morning* by Marc Harshman. Illustration copyright © 1999 by Felipe Dávalos.

Charlesbridge Publishing: Cover illustration from *Different Just Like Me* by Lori Mitchell. Copyright © 1999 by Lori Mitchell.

Childrens Press: Cover illustration by Dennis Hockerman from *The Little Red Hen* by Patricia and Fredrick McKissack. Copyright © 1985 by Regensteiner Publishing Enterprises, Inc.

Clarion Books, a Houghton Mifflin Company imprint: Cover illustration by James Ransome from *Aunt Flossie's Hats (and Crab Cakes Later)* by Elizabeth Fitzgerald Howard. Illustration copyright © 1991 by James Ransome.

HarperCollins Publishers: Cover illustration from *Where the Forest Meets the Sea* by Jeannie Baker. Copyright © 1987 by Jeannie Baker. Cover illustration by Arnold Lobel from *Sam the Minuteman* by Nathaniel G. Benchley. Illustration copyright © 1969 by Arnold Lobel. Cover illustration from *Pelle's New Suit* by Elsa Beskow, translated by Marion Letcher Woodburn. © 1994 by Bonnier Carlsen Bokförlag AB; translation © by HarperCollins Publishers. Originally published in Swedish under the title *Pelles nya Kläder* by Albert Bonniers, Stockholm, 1912. Cover illustration from *All the Colors of the Earth* by Sheila Hamanaka. Copyright © 1994 by Sheila Hamanaka. Cover illustration by Ken Heyman from *Houses and Homes* by Ann Morris. Illustration copyright © 1992 by Ken Heyman. Cover illustration by Felicia Bond from *The Big Green Pocketbook* by Candice Ransom. Illustration copyright © 1993 by Felicia Bond.

Henry Holt and Company, Inc.: Cover illustration from *At the Beach* by Huy Voun Lee. Copyright © 1994 by Huy Voun Lee.

Hyperion Books for Children, an imprint of Disney Children's Books: Cover illustration by Daniel Kirk from *The Diggers* by Margaret Wise Brown. Illustration copyright © 1995 by Daniel Kirk.

Little, Brown and Company (Inc.): Cover illustration from *Taking a Walk/Caminando* by Rebecca Emberley. Copyright © 1990 by Rebecca Emberley.

North-South Books Inc.: Cover illustration by Christopher Manson from *Over the River and Through the Wood* by Lydia Maria Child. Illustration copyright © 1993 by Christopher Manson.

Orchard Books, New York: Cover illustration from *Never Spit on Your Shoes* by Denys Cazet. Copyright © 1990 by Denys Cazet. *The Leaving Morning* by Angela Johnson, illustrated by David Soman. Text copyright © 1992 by Angela Johnson; illustration copyright © 1992 by David Soman.

Random House, Inc.: "Home! You're Where It's Warm Inside" from *The Random House Book of Poetry for Children* by Jack Prelutsky. Text copyright © 1983 by Jack Prelutsky.

Marian Reiner, on behalf of Aileen Fisher: "First Day of School" from *Always Wondering* by Aileen Fisher. Text copyright © 1991 by Aileen Fisher.

Scholastic Australia Pty Ltd.: Cover illustration by Julie Vivas from *Let's Eat* by Ana Zamorano. Illustration copyright © 1996 by Julie Vivas. Originally published by Omnibus Books, a division of the Scholastic Australia Group, 1996.

Schroder Music Co.: Lyrics from "I Live in a City" by Malvina Reynolds. Lyrics © 1960 by Schroder Music Co. (ASCAP), renewed 1988.

Viking Penguin, a division of Penguin Putnam Inc.: Cover illustration from *Crow Boy* by Taro Yashima. Copyright © 1955 by Mitsu and Taro Yashima, renewed 1983 by Taro Yashima.

Albert Whitman & Company: Cover illustration by Diane Paterson from *All Kinds of Children* by Norma Simon. Illustration © 1999 by Diane Paterson.

Wonderland Music Company, Inc.: Lyrics and music from "It's a Small World" by Richard M. Sherman and Robert B. Sherman. Copyright © 1963 by Wonderland Music Company, Inc.; copyright renewed.